Moon Shadow

Moon Shadow

CHRIS PLATT

PEACHTREE
ATLANTA

Ω

Published by
PEACHTREE PUBLISHERS
1700 Chattahoochee Avenue
Atlanta, Georgia 30318-2112

www.peachtree-online.com

Text © 2006 by Chris Platt
Cover illustration © 2006 by Paul Bachem

Cover design by Loraine M. Joyner
Book design by Melanie McMahon Ives

Photos on pp. 163-164 © 2006 Lifesavers, Inc., Wild Horse Rescue

Printed in the United States of America
10 9 8 7 6 5 4 3 2 1
First Edition

Library of Congress Cataloging-in-Publication Data

Platt, Chris, 1959- 182-9617
  Moon shadow / by Chris Platt. – 1st ed.
    p. cm.
  Summary: Thirteen-year-old Callie is determined to save and raise a beautiful but sickly mustang foal after the filly is orphaned in a Nevada desert round-up.
  ISBN 1-56145-382-X
  [1. Horses–Fiction. 2. West (U.S.)–Fiction. 3. Nevada–Fiction.] I. Title.
  PZ7.P7123115Mo 2006
  [Fic]–dc22
                              2006012002

For Betty Dravis,
my good friend and critique partner

Special thanks to my editors at Peachtree
for all their efforts in making this book the best it can be.

One

❦

shrill whinny pierced the quiet of the northern Nevada desert, startling a flock of blue scrub jays into flight. Thirteen-year-old Callie McLean smiled as the pesky birds rose from the sea of gray-green sagebrush, their *ha-ha-ha* caws making a horrible racket.

The mustangs had to be close by.

Callie pushed her straight, sandy-brown hair behind her ears and lowered herself to the ground, crawling on her belly over the top of the rock outcropping. She felt the abrasive rub of sand where her shirt had come untucked. She frowned. Her mother was going to have a fit when she saw the mess she'd made of her new hand-sewn blouse.

Quickly dismissing that thought, Callie edged further onto the rocks that rose fifty feet above the scene unfolding on the valley floor below. She shielded her eyes from the glare of the early-morning sun and watched as a young bay stallion trumpeted his cry once more, pawing at the ground and shaking his head. The bachelor stallion's brown coat and black mane and tail glistened in the sun as he sent out his challenge.

A hundred yards away stood the golden buckskin stallion with the black mane and tail. Callie had named him Cloud Dancer when she first discovered the herd. The little palomino mare she called Moonbeam was close by his side. This was her dream horse. She'd fallen in love with the mare three years ago, when Moonbeam had only been a yearling.

When the little yellow mare turned to the side, she exposed her rounded belly. Callie smiled broadly. Moonbeam was in foal! Her favorite mustang was going to have a baby!

Callie's attention was drawn back to the danger at hand when Cloud Dancer gave a great snort of warning, then spun on his hind legs and rounded up his band of mares and foals. His jet-black mane and tail flowed on the breeze as he circled the herd, nipping at their flanks. Callie knew he was driving them to a safe spot away from the bachelor stallion, but not so far away that yet another stallion could steal his harem while he was doing battle with this competitor.

When Cloud Dancer's mares were out of danger, he turned and answered the young upstart's challenge, giving his own battle cry as he ran to meet the bay.

Callie gasped. The older stud raced toward the other horse and slid to a stop twenty feet from the determined bay. The buckskin pawed the ground as he bowed his neck and flexed his muscles in a display ritual meant to show his dominance. He was giving the younger, less-experienced stallion a chance to back down and run away.

But the bay seemed full of himself, unwilling to accept defeat in advance. He arched his neck until his mane bristled, then pawed at the sand, inviting the larger horse's challenge.

Callie quickly scanned the horizon, spotting the small group of bachelor mustangs to which this insolent bay belonged. They stood several hundred yards away with their ears pricked, waiting for the outcome of the fight.

She smiled. The young male horses were not yet old enough, or strong enough, to fight for mares of their own. They'd been kicked out of their own herds by their sires when they were roughly two years of age. Being herd animals, they banded together for safety and companionship, spending their time playing stallion games of mock battle. They practiced for the day when they'd be strong enough to fight for a herd of their own.

If their brave herd-mate won this battle, they might be able to steal a mare or two from him before he made off with his new harem. If he lost, they would go back to their usual routine of grazing and playing, until they themselves would be ready to challenge the leader of another herd. Only the strongest stallions could command a herd of their own. That was Nature's way of insuring their survival.

Callie waited to see what the stallions would do. Harvey Smith, the old mustanger who worked at the Antelope Springs mustang pens, had been telling her wild horse stories for as long as she could remember. He'd be impressed that today she'd have her own mustang tale to tell.

A loud snort focused Callie's attention on the posturing stallions. The bay was at least two hundred pounds lighter than Cloud Dancer, and he lacked the muscle development of the seasoned stud. If the young horse had any sense, Callie thought, he would hightail it back to the bachelor herd before the buckskin turned him into a noontime snack for the vultures.

The thought sent a chill down Callie's spine. She prayed that the younger mustang would bow out, but it was obvious from the strong stance the bay took in the sand that he was set on earning a band of mares for himself. He gave a belligerent shake of his head and snorted his impatience.

A loud battle cry burst from Cloud Dancer as he rushed to meet the young upstart. He rose on his hind legs and pawed at the bay. The smaller horse met the challenge, flailing his front hooves and baring his teeth.

In an incredible show of speed and agility, Cloud Dancer turned in midair, planted his forelegs, and launched a powerful kick at the bay's exposed belly.

Callie winced as the loud thud echoed off the canyon walls. The young horse snorted in fear and toppled over backwards. Before he could gain his feet, the older stallion came at him with hooves and teeth and grabbed the challenger by the mane, shaking him like a piece of sagebrush in a windstorm.

The young bay gained a foothold in the sand and attempted to stand, but the older stallion turned and blasted him with another kick from his powerful hindquarters. The younger horse was sent sprawling back to the ground.

Callie's stomach did a flip. "Please, stay down," she whispered as she watched the bay colt struggle to rise. She'd heard about stallion fights from old Harvey and the cowboys who worked the pens. If the bay remained on the ground, the old buckskin might let him live. But the arrogant youth staggered to his feet and bared his teeth once more.

Callie groaned. The bay had blown his chance to walk away with some of his pride—and his hide—intact. He had chosen to fight to the death. The young mustang hadn't yet figured out that he was too small and weak to win a fight against this superior horse.

Callie thought about springing from her hiding place and waving her arms in an attempt to break up the fight, but she knew from listening to the hands at the mustang pens that it wouldn't be a good idea. The wild stallion might see her as just another challenger, and treat her the same way he did the bay.

After all her years of living in the high desert and studying the wild firsthand, Callie knew better than to get in the way of Mother Nature. Out here it was survival of the fittest. The stronger stallion would win this fight and earn his right to sire next year's crop of foals. The weak stallions died, or limped off to gather their strength and try again later. Those were the rules, and it wasn't her place to break them. It might be difficult to watch a horse be killed or maimed in a fight, but if a lesser stallion was allowed to breed, it would create a weaker crop of foals. Only the strongest could survive out here in the wild.

Callie sucked in her breath when Cloud Dancer rose on his hind legs once again. He dove at the smaller horse, sinking his teeth into his shoulder and ripping a large chunk of his hide. The bay screamed in agony as the next kick sent him tumbling into the sand. He lay on the ground, his sweat-slicked coat glistening in the sun. His rib cage rose and fell with each labored breath.

Callie watched the old stud circle the young horse, snorting with gusto as he pranced and tossed his head, daring the weaker horse to rise again.

The smell of dust mixed with sage floated up to assault

Callie's nostrils. She pinched her nose to stop a sneeze that might startle the old stallion and cause him to attack the younger horse again.

In the distance, Cloud Dancer's mares and the bachelor herd stood at opposite sides of the valley, heads raised. They were awaiting the outcome.

Callie gripped the edge of the outcropping, ignoring the pain in her fingers as the rough rocks bit into her flesh. She knew this was the way of the wild, but she hated to see a beautiful animal die such a brutal death. She hoped that the bay stallion would remain in his prone position. If he rose, Cloud Dancer would surely kill him.

The grunts and ragged breathing of the exhausted horse floated up from below. Callie let out a sigh of relief as the younger mustang twitched and lifted his head to nicker at his conqueror before lowering his muzzle back to the sand in complete surrender.

The buckskin did a victory dance, bowing his neck and prancing around the defeated youngster before trumpeting a call to the mares. With a toss of his head, he turned and raced toward them. Moonbeam was the first to greet the victorious stallion. The golden palomino stepped forward and touched noses with her mate. The other mares accepted him into the fold with anxious nickers. Then the herd turned as a unit and sprinted over the next ridge.

Callie rose to her feet, keeping her eye on the still form of the vanquished bay as she made her way down the hillside, clutching the bitterbrush for support. The sand and rocks rolled beneath her boots as she quickly descended to the bottom.

With her heart in her throat, she quietly covered the distance between her and the young mustang. As she drew closer, her palms began to sweat. She knew better than to get this close to a wild horse. It didn't matter that the little bay had just been defeated in battle and was seriously injured. He might still be strong enough to hurt a human—especially a young girl. If Harvey or her parents knew she was doing this, she'd be grounded for life.

The bay mustang lay in the clearing. Blood ran down his foam-flecked coat; his sides heaved from exertion. Callie stopped thirty yards from him, glad to see that he was still breathing. She was surprised that she was able to venture so close. As loud as her heart was beating, she was sure he'd be able to hear it.

She wished there was something she could do to help the wounded stallion, but she didn't dare try to touch him. Wild horses often struck out in defense. One blow of a powerful hoof could break bones, or even kill.

"Come on, boy, you can make it," Callie crooned. "You're young and healthy. This isn't your day to die." She kept her voice low as she edged several feet closer.

The mustang lifted his head and snorted. Callie took a few more steps and the horse bolted to his feet, blowing a warning snort as he hobbled back to his herd on unsteady legs. After several rounds of greetings and an inspection by the bravest bachelor of the bunch, they wandered off in the opposite direction, distancing themselves from the reigning buckskin's herd.

Callie brushed her dirty hands on her jeans as she watched them go. Soon it would be someone else's turn to challenge the leader. The band of bachelors would gather their courage, and another young stud would fight for the coveted position of leader of Cloud Dancer's band.

She shielded her eyes and peered through the settling dust kicked up by the horses. The bachelor herd disappeared over the hill, and there was nothing left but silence. She glanced at her watch. Her friend Billie was coming to visit at ten o'clock.

Callie picked up the old, pieced-together mountain bike she had stashed in the bitterbrush and pedaled toward home. She couldn't wait to share her story with Billie. Especially the part about seeing her dream horse, Moonbeam.

Two

⁕

allie extinguished the sickeningly sweet incense sticks that her mother had left burning in the holder on the table. *Old hippies.* That's what the kids at school called her parents. And unfortunately, her classmates believed in guilt by association. The tie-dyed shirts and seventies-style vests and blouses that her mother sewed for her to wear to school brought on more teasing than she cared to put up with. At least school was out for the summer. That meant three months of freedom, beginning with this morning's ride with Billie.

She opened a window of their rickety old farmhouse and fanned the curtains to help the cloying smell escape. Billie would be here any minute, and the smell always made her best friend feel a bit nauseated. Callie didn't care for the odor much herself, but she was so used to it she hardly noticed it any more.

Celah, the family's Percheron draft horse, lifted her head and snorted. Callie leaned out the window and spoke to the large black mare that stood in the paddock nearby. "Hey, I know you don't like the scent any more than I do, but there's more fresh air out there to dissipate it."

Callie frowned as she ducked back through the window. There she went again, using a two-dollar word when a fifty-cent one would do. *Dissipate.* She could imagine Luke Thompson, a boy from school who lived a mile down the road, heckling her now.

Hey, Miss Smarty-pants, I bet you don't even know what that big word means!

Callie ran a hand through her tangled hair and blew an exasperated breath through her bangs. She couldn't help it that she was smart—or for that matter, that Luke was so dumb.

She grinned to herself. If her mother knew she was thinking such mean thoughts, she would give Callie an extra load of chores to do.

If you can't say anything nice, don't say anything at all, her mother always said.

Callie stared at her scratched-up, callused hands, remembering the five wheelbarrow loads of weeds she'd had to pull from the organic vegetable garden the last time she'd made a rude comment about somebody.

She snipped a piece of aloe plant and smeared it across her scratches. She would just have to learn to keep her thoughts to herself when her mother was around. Especially comments about Luke. Her mother liked to keep things friendly with the neighbors.

Callie wished that Billie lived next door, but her friend's parents owned a large house at the edge of the nearest big town, almost ten miles away. She'd met her when they'd both been placed in an advanced English class, and their love of horses had drawn them together. Billie had desperately wanted a horse, but her family didn't have a place to keep one. Not long after Callie's parents had offered the Simmonses a chance to board on their property, however, Billie had become the proud new owner of a beautiful red chestnut mare she named Star.

During the school year, Billie was only allowed to come out on Saturdays. But now that it was summer break, Callie hoped her friend would be able to visit several times a week.

A horn blasted and Callie leaned back out the window to see Billie step from her father's new truck. Callie figured Mr. Simmons probably paid more for that pickup than her parents made in a whole year.

"I'll be out in a minute!" Callie hollered. "Star's in the barn. I put your saddle on the rack next to the tack room."

Billie nodded and hurried toward the barn. "Don't be long," she called over her shoulder. "I might leave without you!" She laughed as she disappeared into the old wooden structure.

Callie grabbed her boots from the corner, hopping on one foot, then the other, as she struggled to get them on. She ran out the front door and headed toward the barn, waving to Billie's father as he pulled out of the driveway.

Callie dearly loved her parents, but sometimes she wondered what it would be like to have parents like Billie's—people with *normal* jobs. Her own mother and father weren't exactly nine-to-five business folks. They didn't want to be bothered by the constraints of punching a time clock, so they grew their own food, raised their own meat, and took odd jobs here and there when their organic vegetable business was slow.

Callie sighed. Both of her parents had college degrees. Why did they have to choose organic farming? Other jobs paid better and were steady. Their small, ancient farmhouse and the old tractor parts that littered their yard were a constant source of embarrassment for her. All the other ranches around here were large spreads with well-to-do owners. Their little patch of ground was like a thorn among the roses.

That was part of why she liked Billie so much. Her friend didn't care that their house sometimes looked like the local junkyard, or that her parents didn't have a lot of money.

Callie admired Billie, too. Her friend was tall and willowy, with shoulder-length blonde hair and a face that made all the boys smile. She was easy-going and quick to make friends. But since they had met at the beginning of the year, Billie had been spending more and more time with Callie and less time with her popular friends. It was the horses, Callie supposed. But whatever the reason, she was glad that Billie had chosen to be her best friend.

She ran her faded bandana under the cool water of the faucet near the barn and tied it around her neck. It was time to quit thinking about school and bothersome stuff like that. It was the second week of June in Antelope Springs, and her vacation had started! Already the sun was blazing its way to a hot summer.

She grabbed Celah's oversized red halter off the post and whistled for the eighteen-hand, two-thousand pound draft mare. The ground practically shook when the big black horse came trotting up to the fence. Callie stood on the top board and slid the halter over Celah's head, then climbed down to open the gate. The gentle mare nuzzled her shirt for a treat while she waited for Callie to undo the gate latch.

"Sorry, girl. No carrots this morning," Callie said as she

walked Celah through an opening that was almost too small for the big draft horse to fit through. "I've got some apples in the barn you can have while we're getting you ready." She patted the mare on the neck, marveling at how gentle she was. Most draft horses had a very calm nature. *It's a good thing,* Callie thought as she looked up at the tall horse. A bad-tempered animal the size of a small car would be a danger to everyone.

Billie was just placing her silver-edged saddle onto Star's back when Callie entered the barn with Celah in tow. The little chestnut mare nickered to the big black, and Celah returned the greeting, practically shaking the rafters with her loud whinny.

Billie stepped back as Callie tied Celah to the hitching post. "Star looks like a Shetland pony compared to this big monster," she said, laughing. "If you ever fall off out in the desert, we'll never be able to get you back up on her again."

Callie smiled. "Believe me when I tell you that I don't plan to fall off anywhere. I don't want to spend the rest of my summer in traction."

There were times when Callie wished she had a smaller horse, one that she could take care of and ride any time she wanted to, but her parents needed the draft mare to pull the garden plow any time the tractor broke down. And besides, she kind of liked being up high enough to see over the tall scrub when she rode out on the desert.

Billie pulled a piece of carrot from her pocket and held it flat-handed under Celah's nose. Star gave a nicker of protest. "You've got to learn to share with your friends," Billie admonished her horse as she watched the carrot instantly disappear into Celah's mouth.

"Guess what?" Callie said excitedly as she pulled the round metal currycomb with the wooden handle from the brush box. She stood on a bucket so she could reach her horse's back. "I saw Cloud Dancer's herd in the desert this morning, and Moonbeam was with him. She's going to have a foal!"

"A baby mustang?" Billie stopped brushing Star and slapped Callie a high-five. "I can't wait! Maybe we'll get to see it right after it's born."

Callie moved the bucket to the other side of the horse and curried up under Celah's mane. "It's going to be the most beautiful foal ever," she said dreamily. "I want to ride back over there and see if we can find the herd."

"Sounds good to me," Billie said. She slipped the bit between her horse's teeth and waited for Callie to finish.

Callie ran the soft brush over Celah's shining ebony coat, then placed the bareback pad onto the mare's broad back. Her family didn't own a saddle, but she was saving her allowance to buy one. She hoped to earn enough doing chores for the neighbors to buy a nice used saddle by the end of the summer.

"Come on, slowpoke," Billie said as she handed Celah's bridle to Callie and helped her get the bit between the mare's teeth.

Callie pulled the bridle over Celah's large head and made sure her mane was straight under the brow band. "Come on, old girl," she said, stepping down from the bucket.

She led the horse out the door and coaxed her over to a stack of hay. The draft mare was almost six feet tall at the withers. There was no way Callie could get on her without standing on something. She climbed onto the hay pile and nimbly vaulted onto the mare's broad back, then smiled at her friend. "It's just like riding an overstuffed couch."

Billie chuckled. "Yeah, except if you fall off a couch, the floor's only a foot away. Falling off Celah would be more like jumping out of the loft of your barn."

"True," Callie said as they turned their mounts onto the sand trail that would lead them over the mountain to the wild mustangs' summer grazing area.

She asked Celah for an easy trot. As they traveled the sandy trails, Callie looked out across the valley. A lot of people thought the Nevada high desert was ugly, but she loved this place. The beauty was there if you just took the time to look. Spring brought colorful, tiny desert wildflowers, and she'd seen sunsets so magnificent that Van Gogh would have been jealous.

Northern Nevada was not the land of tall grass and massive forests. It was an area of frugal beauty and harsh environments that could see temperatures of over 100 degrees during the daytime and temperatures below freezing at night. This land could make or break both man and beast.

Sparse tufts of green grass sprouted here and there among the peach blossom, bitterbrush, and sage. A few scraggly pinion pines dotted the outer edges of the flatlands and the sides of the hills and mountains. It wasn't what most folks would call good grazing land, but it was all the mustangs had. And they had to share this small bit of forage with the cattle and sheep the big ranches turned out on the federal grazing lands.

Unlike other states, 85 percent of Nevada was owned by the United States government. The Bureau of Land Management, or BLM, was responsible for watching over these precious lands and keeping everything in balance.

Callie frowned. It was a never-ending battle. The ranchers claimed that the mustangs had overpopulated the area and were eating up all the grass that should be going to fatten their livestock. Animal rights organizations like WHOA and Wild Horse Spirit argued that the mustangs were American's natural heritage and needed to be protected.

Billie pulled Star alongside the big draft mare. "Hey, what are you thinking about?" she said. "School's out, remember? We don't have to think any brilliant thoughts for the rest of summer."

Callie grinned sheepishly. "Want to hear about the stallion fight I saw this morning?" she said.

"A fight?"

"Yes, and a pretty bad one, too."

Billie took off her straw hat and fanned herself. "You're so lucky," she said. "I can't believe you actually got to see a fight! How'd you get that close?"

Callie scanned the horizon, searching for any movement that might indicate a wild bunch. "There's a place I found with a great view into the valley where the horses like to graze. It's got a lot of sagebrush and big boulders to hide behind. As long as you keep quiet, the herd goes about its daily—" She stopped in mid-sentence and glanced over her shoulder, sure that she had seen something moving.

"Anyway," she went on, turning her attention back to Billie, "I saw the mustangs early this morning. One of the young bachelor stallions thought he was tough enough to challenge Cloud Dancer."

Billie let out a low whistle. "Big mistake."

Callie nodded. "Yeah. As far as I can figure, that bay is about four or five years old, not really a colt anymore." Old Harvey had told her that a male horse was called a colt until the end of his fourth year. After that, he could be called a stallion. "But he has more courage than brains, I think."

"Cloud Dancer's built like a tank and he's tough as Luke Thompson's head," Billie said. "Did the bay live through it?"

Callie glanced behind her again. The hair on the back of her neck prickled. She couldn't shake the feeling that they were being watched. She turned back to her friend. "Yeah, but he was pretty banged up."

Billie sighed. "I wish I could have been there. I never get to see anything like that."

Callie squeezed her legs against Celah's sides, urging her to walk up beside Billie's mare. The draft mare was a little on the lazy side and tended to lag behind if Callie wasn't paying attention. "Stallion fights are not a pretty sight," she said. "The bay that fought this morning was badly hurt, and I think his spirit was broken. It'll probably be a long time before he challenges the buckskin again."

"What happens if a stallion is never strong enough to gather a herd of his own?" Billie asked.

Callie shrugged. "Sometimes a lesser stallion will come upon a young filly that's been kicked out of her herd, or maybe an old mare that nobody wants. Then he'll have his own herd for a while, until a stronger stallion steals her away. But usually, only the strongest males can gather and protect a herd long enough to sire a new crop of foals."

The sensation of being spied upon ran up Callie's spine again. She looked around, but still saw nothing that would cause her alarm. "The mustang territory is just over this hill," she said. "Let's canter."

Callie clucked to Celah and grabbed a large handful of mane as she prepared for the mare's takeoff. Everything Celah did was big. The Percheron jolted to a start and followed behind Billie's sleek mare.

Billie laughed as they followed a deer trail through the sagebrush. "I can't believe how much noise Celah makes when her feet hit the ground."

Callie smiled. Riding Celah was like riding an elephant. She felt like they could go through anything. But as big as the mare was, she had surprisingly smooth gaits—a good thing since Callie didn't ride with a saddle.

She wondered what it would be like to ride a horse like Cloud Dancer, or her palomino mare, Moonbeam. How would it feel to glide over the ground at the speed of the wind instead of the slow, steady canter of the draft mare?

They pulled the horses back to a walk as they topped the next rise. Celah was blowing hard from the exertion of hauling her large body up the incline. Callie patted the mare and jumped from her back.

"We better tie the horses up here," Callie said, pointing to a heavy clump of sage. "We've got to crawl to the edge of the rocks. If any mustangs down below see us, they'll bolt." Callie tied Celah off, then got down on her hands and knees and clambered onto the outcrop, reminding herself not to wreck another one of her mom's handmade shirts.

Billie edged up beside Callie on the flat rock outcropping. "Are they there?" she asked. "What about Moonbeam? You've told me so much, I can't wait to see her. I bet she's beautiful."

Callie brought a finger to her lips to silence her friend, then pointed to the band of wild horses below. There were eight mares of varying colors. Cloud Dancer seemed to prefer lighter colored mares, like Moonbeam, but there was at least one black in the herd, and one bay. Several of the mares had last season's yearlings tagging along, while a couple of the younger mares nursed new foals.

Callie pointed a finger at the palomino. "That's her," she said. "I call her Moonbeam because she's such a pale shade of yellow. Look how big her belly is. I bet she doesn't have too much longer to wait before she foals."

"She *is* beautiful." Billie's voice held a note of awe.

"I wish she were mine," Callie said wistfully.

A loud snort from Cloud Dancer jolted the silence. Callie wondered if the stallion had sensed they were there. But a moment later, a loud human shout sounded from the bottom of the valley about a half-mile away.

Cloud Dancer urged the herd into a run. He wanted to get his new foals and pregnant mare away from the danger. After the herd was safely on its way, the stallion turned to face the intruder, assessing the danger. Experience had taught him that it was better to avoid the challenge of a screaming human on horseback. The stallion spun on his heels and galloped after his harem.

"Wh...what's going on?" Billie sputtered as the rider galloped across the valley below. "Isn't that Luke Thompson? What's he doing out here?"

Callie stared in disbelief as she shaded her eyes and watched her young neighbor give chase to the mustang herd. She stood and planted clenched fists on her hips. "Darn his ignorant hide! What does he think he's doing?"

The boy spotted them standing on the hill and pulled his blue-roan quarter horse to a sliding stop, forcing the gelding into a practiced rear. He tipped his hat in the girls' direction before he cantered up the hill toward them.

Billie dusted off her jeans and frowned at the approaching rider. "How'd he know we were here?"

Callie shrugged. "I had a feeling someone was following us, ever since we left the house. It must have been him."

Luke stopped his horse beside the two mares. He swept his hat from his head and mock-bowed low over his gelding's withers. "Mustanger Luke at your service, ladies."

"Of all the stupid things…" Callie picked up a handful of pebbles, intending to bounce a few off the boy's thick skull, but she thought better of it. She didn't want to have to haul the fool back to her house if she hurt him. "What do you think you're doing?" she demanded angrily.

Luke opened his mouth to speak, but his answer was lost on the wind as a loud *chop, chop, chop* echoed through the hills. A second later, a small black-and-white helicopter broke over the rise, raising dust and creating a racket.

Luke's gelding jumped out from under him, tossing the arrogant boy into the brush. Callie would have laughed if she hadn't been so busy trying to get hold of Celah. Billie ran to get Star, but the two mares broke their tie ropes at the same time. They turned and cantered toward home with their manes and tails flying on the wind.

The helicopter passed out of range. Luke groaned as he untangled his long legs and rose from the spiky bush, dusting off his pants. The girls watched all three horses disappear over the hill.

"What do we do now?" Billie said in dismay, looking to Callie.

"I guess we have no choice." Callie glared at Luke. "Unless Mr. Mustanger here has his cell phone so he can call his dad to come pick us up in his four-wheel drive, it looks like we're going to be walking home." She brushed past Luke and started down the trail. It was going to be a hot, dusty two miles back to her house.

Three

T hat was awesome!" Luke said, pulling the hat off his sweaty brow.

Callie ignored him and continued to march homeward. Her boots were pinching her feet and she could feel a blister forming on her heel with each step she took.

Billie kept pace with Callie. "Who do you think that chopper belonged to?" she asked. "I don't remember ever seeing anyone out here when we were riding."

"I don't know." Callie kept her voice low so as not to invite a three-way conversation, but Luke pushed between them. Callie glared at him. "I was too busy trying to catch Celah to get much of a look at the copter, but it looked like the ones the Bureau of Land Management uses. Their logo isn't very big, so it's hard to tell."

Luke grabbed a lock of Callie's unruly hair and gave it a teasing tug. "Oh, come on, why would the BLM be out here?" He reached down to pluck a long stem of wild grass and stuck it between his teeth. "There's nothing here to manage but sagebrush and jackrabbits."

Callie ignored him and directed her answer to Billie. "They're probably looking over the mustang herds, getting ready to do a roundup. Harvey said he heard them talking in the office back at the adoption center. He's not too keen on helicopter roundups. It's really hard on the horses."

As they tromped across the sand, a hollow pit opened in the bottom of Callie's stomach. *What if they round up Cloud Dancer's herd?* she thought. It really bothered her that Moonbeam could be gathered in the pens and put up for adoption. Callie knew that she'd saved almost enough from her allowance to cover the $125 adoption fee, but Moonbeam would have her foal soon, and her parents wouldn't be able to pay for the everyday upkeep of two horses.

She took a deep breath and told herself not to worry. Cloud Dancer had been grazing these valleys with his mares for years and he'd always kept his herd safe. He had produced a legacy of beautiful wild foals that would roam the hills for many more years to come.

"I'll call Harvey when we get home and see if he knows anything more," Callie said. "Hopefully, they're just doing a head count."

Luke gave Billie a toothy grin. "They haven't done any roundups out here for a long time," he said, trying to show off his knowledge of horses. "They're not allowed to use the chopper in the spring because it's foaling season. After June, they can use the helicopter to round up the horses and drive them over long distances."

"But your mustang is still in foal," Billie said to Callie. "What will happen to Moonbeam if they do a roundup?"

Seeing the warning look on Callie's face, Luke threw an arm over each girl's shoulder, dragging them to a slower pace. "Callie's mustang?" he asked as he looked from one to the other. "Ha! Callie doesn't own a mustang mare. The only thing she's got is that big tank she passes off as a horse. She ought to get herself a real horse, like one of our registered quarter horses."

Callie shrugged out of his grasp. "Okay, that's it!" she said with a stomp of her foot that she knew probably seemed childish. "You're not fit company for a vulture, Luke. This is where we part ways."

"I agree," Billie said, crossing her arms over her chest.

Luke put up a hand. "Hey, two against one isn't fair." When he saw that his protest didn't faze the girls, he gave up. "All right, I'm leaving. Don't go gettin' yourselves so riled up. I was only joking."

Callie fought the urge to yell out something mean as Luke stumbled down the side of the hill and picked up the trail that led to his father's ranch. *How dare he insult Celah!* Callie thought. She's a great mare. So what if she's not tiny and sleek like the Thompsons' fancy quarter horses?

"Don't pay any attention to him," Billie said. "He just likes to get a rise out of you."

Callie took a deep, stuttering breath and sighed in exasperation. "Well, it worked. What a brat! Why can't he just leave me alone? He always picks on me."

Billie hooked her arm through Callie's and steered her back up the trail. "My little brother's the same way," she said. "He just wants attention, and he doesn't care what he has to do to get it. Look at all the trouble Luke gets into at school. Besides..." Billie said hesitantly. "This is going to sound crazy, but I think maybe he likes you."

Callie rolled her eyes. Who in their right mind would want a boyfriend like that? "Well, somebody better tell him he's got an odd way of showing it. He always makes fun of what I do or say, or the clothes I wear." She plucked at a ribbon her mother had sewn onto her shirt. "It's not my fault my mother makes weird clothes and expects me to wear them."

They walked in silence for a few steps. "What about that great warm wheat bread and fresh blackberry jam your mom makes?" Billie said. "I'm kind of jealous. My mother never makes anything by hand."

Callie felt a little bit better. Who really cared what Luke Thompson thought anyway?

"All the girls at school think he's cute," Billie said. "I could name a dozen of them who'd love to have Luke ask them to a dance or something."

"Yuck!" Callie said. "They obviously don't know him like we do. Luke reminds me of that big old roping horse his dad has."

"How's that?" Billie asked with a curious lift of her brow.

"Well, he's one of the most beautiful horses on the place," Callie said. "But he's so ornery that nobody can stand to be around him."

The girls laughed together as they turned down the path that led to Callie's house.

Callie glanced at her watch. "Oh no! Dr. Susan is supposed to pick me up at one o'clock. We're doing sick pen today."

"I think it's so cool that a real vet is letting you help with the mustangs at the adoption center," Billie said, picking up the pace. "It's even better that you're getting extra class credit for summer work."

Callie ignored her sore feet and broke into a jog. She'd always wanted to be a vet, mostly because she loved animals. But it didn't hurt any that veterinarians also made good money. Someday, when she grew up, she planned to own a place where she could have as many horses as she wanted.

"My parents thought that working with Dr. Susan would give me a good idea of what I'm in for if I become a vet," Callie explained. "Sometimes the work is kind of messy and unpleasant. If I can keep from fainting at the sight of a needle or the sound of scissors cutting into a live animal's hide, I just might make it."

"Eww," Billie said. "I just couldn't do it. I don't have a strong enough stomach."

As they topped the last rise that was directly behind Callie's house, they were surprised to see the McLeans trudging up the incline.

"Thank goodness, you're not hurt!" Callie's mother ran up and threw her arms around the two girls.

Mr. McLean stopped to catch his breath. "When the horses came back alone, we feared the worst. What happened?"

Callie stared at her parents. Her mother's tie-dyed shirts and her father's long, braided hair might make them look different from other parents, but there was one thing Callie could always count on: They loved her. She hugged them both. "A helicopter spooked the horses. We had to walk back."

"Must be roundup time," Sarah McLean said as she tucked a lock of her daughter's hair behind her ear and smoothed her bangs. "Better hurry. Susan's waiting for you."

Callie looked at her friend. She didn't want to just walk out on her, but Billie shooed her on.

"You get going," she said. "I'll make sure Star and Celah are all right. My dad will be here soon to pick me up, anyway."

Callie gave Billie and her parents a smile of thanks and ran down the hill toward the house and Dr. Susan.

❧

The veterinarian was sitting in her little white pickup. Dr. Susan had been the family's equine vet ever since Callie could remember. Everything about the petite brunette—from her neat bobbed haircut to the wire-rimmed glasses perched on the end of her nose—was very businesslike.

"Hi, Susan," Callie said as she grabbed her tennis shoes from the porch and jumped into the pickup. She buckled herself into the passenger seat and waved to her parents and Billie as the vehicle pulled away from the house.

"I see you've got another old tractor out back," Susan said. She adjusted her rearview mirror and pushed her glasses up further on her nose.

"Yeah, my dad says he's going to use it for parts to fix our good tractor," Callie said. "I sure hope he can, because if he doesn't get it to work, he'll have to hitch Celah up to the plow, and I won't be able to do much riding this summer." She stared out the window at the vast Nevada landscape and sighed. "I just wish my parents would figure out what century the rest of us are living in."

Callie fidgeted in her seat. She could feel Susan's kind brown eyes on her.

"Your parents are good people, Callie. Don't be so hard on them."

Callie's cheeks grew warm as she nodded in agreement. She felt like a traitor for speaking about her parents like that.

They spent the rest of the short ride in silence. The vet pulled into the dirt driveway of the Antelope Springs mustang pens and parked next to the long stack of alfalfa that ran the entire length of the corrals.

Callie got out and looked around. She loved the view from up here. The blue bowl of a sky touched the greening hills on all sides of the valley. A pair of red-tailed hawks circled lazily on the thermals, while below, a lone jackrabbit darted from sagebrush to sagebrush.

"I hear the new cowboy arrived today," Susan said as she stepped from the pickup. "They say he's got a son about your age, maybe a year older."

Callie shrugged. If the boy was like Luke, she didn't want anything to do with him.

A soft nicker drew Callie's attention toward the stock pens. The cowboys who worked for the BLM kept their horses in the front lot, but she could see several smaller horses milling around in the middle corrals.

The captured mustangs were mainly bays and chestnuts, but there were a few pintos and duns in the bunch. Their short backs and pointed fox ears denoted the classic look of the Spanish barb horses that the conquistadors had left behind when they returned to Spain four centuries ago. Though the mustangs had an intense distrust of humans, their curious nature brought them closer to the fence to see what was happening.

"Let's go, Callie," Susan called. "We've got some sick ones to treat. Grab my bag and meet me at the squeeze chute."

As Callie retrieved the bag from the vet's truck, she thought she heard the low *thup thup thup* of a helicopter. But the sound quickly vanished against the rushing hoofbeats of the wild horses being herded into the sick pen.

From the looks of things, Callie and the vet would have their hands full for the next couple of hours. Callie figured there'd be plenty of time later to fret about a roundup. But as she toted the medical bag over to the vet, she couldn't help but worry about Moonbeam and her coming foal. Surely the noise of the helicopter was disturbing the mare in a time when she needed peace and quiet.

Four

The new man and his son were waiting for Dr. Susan and Callie at the sick pen.

"Good afternoon," Susan said.

The older cowboy tipped his hat. "Afternoon, ma'am, miss. My name's Sam Rosser. This here's my son, Justin."

Callie looked up at the tall gangly teenager with the blondish-red hair sitting astride a handsome black-and-white paint gelding. The boy seemed kind of shy. What was his name again? She hadn't heard it clearly. "Um, Gus?" she asked.

The young cowboy looked annoyed. He plucked his black Stetson hat from where it rested on the horn of his saddle and plopped it on top of his head. "That's *Jus*-tin," he said, enunciating the word for her like she might be a little slow. He reined his gelding in a half circle and stood beside his father's mount.

Callie stared at the ground, a slow burn coming to her cheeks. "Sorry," she mumbled, feeling like an idiot. She didn't even know this boy, and already he was upset with her. Who could ever understand boys?

Susan stepped forward and shook the man's hand. "I'm Dr. Susan. I'm the official vet for the mustang pens." She pointed to Callie. "This is my assistant, Callie McLean."

Callie decided to ignore Justin. She nodded to Mr. Rosser and then climbed up on the green metal bars of the corral fence, surveying the mustangs within. The wild horses huddled at the opposite end, snorting in fear of the humans around them. "Easy, easy," Callie crooned, already forgetting Justin. "We're here to make you better so someone will adopt you."

She stepped down from the fence. She was sure the mustangs didn't want to be adopted. They'd rather be out on the range running free. But they had been captured, and now it was their fate. People came from all over the United States to adopt a piece of the "Old West." Callie hoped that each horse would at least get a good home.

She remembered a recent newspaper article suggesting that some mustangs were being sold to slaughterhouses. Officials of the BLM had gone in to check on a particular group of sale animals whose brands had been altered. The mustangs had been rescued, but the man who'd sold them couldn't be found.

Old Harvey suspected that Ron Jeffers, the boss man, knew something about the guy who had committed the crime, but Harvey admitted that it was only speculation.

"Cut me out that bay with the bad leg," Susan called to Sam.

Callie admired the swift work of Sam's cow pony as he wheeled on his hind legs and moved toward his target, cutting the bay from the rest of the herd, then driving the injured mustang into the chute while Justin's horse held the others back.

Once the animal was in place, the gate was closed to prevent him from backing out. The squeeze chute folded in until the panicked animal was gripped snugly within the walls. Held in this way, the wild horse couldn't move to injure himself, or the veterinarian.

"Hand me the bucket of Betadine wash, and grab the bottle of antibiotic, Callie," Susan instructed as she probed the wound on the mustang's leg. The horse snorted in fear, but he remained in the same position while the vet worked quickly and efficiently to clean the wound. When Susan was finished, the next animal was herded into the chute and the process was repeated.

Callie heard the distant sound of the helicopter again and turned toward the mountains. The cowboys were gazing in that direction, too.

Susan looked up from the barbed wire wound she was cleansing. "You have some new horses coming in today, boys?"

Sam nodded and pulled a piece of hay from between his lips. "That's one of our guys out there in the chopper. Soon as they get a little closer, me and my son are gonna go on out and bring 'em in the rest of the way."

"I hear they've got some pretty nice horses coming in," Justin said from the back of his saddle horse.

Callie was surprised to see his eyes light up at the mention of the new horses. Did he approve of the roundups, or was he just excited about seeing new mustangs?

Sam smoothed his thick mustache and scowled. "You better wait around when you're done with this bunch, doc. They've been driving those mustangs with the helicopter, and there's always a few of them pretty banged up, or ready to drop from exhaustion."

Susan sighed. "I liked it better in the old days, when they rounded them up by horse."

Sam tipped his hat. "Me, too, but you know progress..." He shrugged.

Progress? Callie almost snorted. Harvey had told her about some of the air roundups in the southern half of the state, where mustangs were driven through fences, or run so hard for so long without water that entire herds were lost. She tightened her lips and stared at the nearby hills. She hoped the incoming horses would be all right.

"Hand me that shot on the tray over there, Callie," Susan said. "This horse has a nasty eye infection."

Callie placed the small gauge needle and syringe in the vet's outstretched palm. She watched as the vet carefully inserted the needle into the corner of the mustang mare's eye.

Callie's stomach tightened. She willed herself not to look away from the needle as it slid slowly into the pink flesh at the corner of the horse's eye. She sucked in a large gulp of air and felt the ground roll beneath her trembling legs. She saw Justin eye her curiously.

I will not faint. I will not faint, Callie repeated to herself as she staggered backwards, grabbing onto a fence rail for support. Everything around her grew dark and tiny dots of light jumped about on the air. Her stomach flopped in protest and her breath came in short, dog-like pants. Her body temperature felt like it had dropped ten degrees, but she could feel the sheen of sweat that popped out on her forehead. She bent over and rested her forehead on the rail.

"Are you all right, Callie?" Susan pulled the release on the chute and the mustang mare stumbled away, shaking her head.

Callie found her voice, but it sounded high-pitched and forced in her own ears. "Yeah, I just need to get a drink of water." She ran her tongue around the inside of her mouth. It felt like she was carrying a big wad of cotton in her cheeks.

"Go on up to the office," Sam said. "There's a stand of cold bottled water up there. Help yourself."

Avoiding Justin's stare, Callie smiled her thanks and hurried toward the main building. She lurched up the office steps and went in, glad to be out of the sun for a minute. As soon as her eyes adjusted to the dim light, she spotted the water cooler in the corner. She filled a Dixie cup and gulped down the cool liquid. It wasn't until the fourth cup that she finally began to taste it. It was the best water she'd ever had.

Callie wiped her mouth with the back of her hand and looked out the window toward the pen where the vet was working. She rubbed her forehead. How could she ever expect to be a veterinarian when she couldn't even *watch* a shot being given? She crumpled up her water cup and threw it in the trash can, shaking her head in disgust. She was such a wimp! And now the new boy knew it, too. Callie took a deep breath and marched back to the sick pen.

She scanned the horizon. The men were heading up the hillside on their cow ponies with an unsaddled horse in tow. They were met at the top of the hill by several more men on horseback. By now she could clearly hear the steady beat of the helicopter as it neared the mustang pens.

Callie climbed to the top rail of the fence to get a better view. "What's the extra horse for?" she asked.

"That's Hank," Susan explained. "He's an old mustang they broke to saddle a long time ago." The vet joined Callie on the fence. "When they get close to the pens, they'll turn Hank loose and he'll go to the front of the line and lead the mustangs right into the corrals."

"Wow." Callie kept her eyes glued to the horizon, waiting for the herd to break over the ridge. "How many do you think are coming?"

"Could be as small a herd as ten," Susan said. "But it might be as high as forty or fifty horses from several herds."

Callie pointed to the cloud of dust on the mountain. "Here they come!"

She watched in awe as the mustangs topped the ridge and raced down the hill toward them. The helicopter hung back, giving the men on horseback a chance to take over. Callie tried to do a head count, but the dust raised from the running herd made it impossible.

Every now and then, she caught a glimpse of the new boy. He rode well. She wished she could be out there, too, riding as fast as the wind beside the racing herd of mustangs.

As the horses drew near, she could feel as well as hear the thundering of the mustangs' hooves as they pounded down the mountainside, their manes and tails flying. One daring animal made a break from the herd. Callie wondered if the horse sensed that captivity lay ahead. She shaded her eyes with her hand and squinted into the sun.

The rays glinted off a golden back as the escapee tossed its black mane and turned to face the cowpoke who had been sent to drive him back into the herd.

Cloud Dancer!

Callie gripped the fence rail and watched as the brave stallion arrogantly challenged his enemy. The cowboy let out a whoop and pulled his lasso from the saddle.

Cloud Dancer tossed his head and neighed to the wild herd, then snorted and spun on his heels, heading for the mountains from which he had just been routed. The cowboy gave chase, but the mustang's fleet hooves and knowledge of the desert served him well. With an oath that Callie could hear from the fence, the man brought his horse to a sliding stop and returned to help with the roundup.

Several of Cloud Dancer's mares tried to follow him, but the cowboys turned them back into the herd and kept them moving toward the mustang pens.

Callie let out a long, slow breath. Was the rest of the stallion's harem in this bunch of captured horses? Was Moonbeam somewhere in the crowd? She strained her eyes, trying to find her favorite mare, but there was too much chaos to be able to pick her out.

As the wild mustangs neared the pens, Hank took his place at the front of the herd and galloped toward the open gate. Callie desperately wanted to slam the gate closed and wave the horses back to their rangeland, but that was impossible.

She'd heard the cowboys talking about the problems with mustangs. When then-President Nixon signed the mustang protection bill into law in 1971, it became a federal offense to harass or kill a wild horse. But the mustangs had to be managed somehow. It was the Bureau of Land Management's responsibility to round up excess horses for adoption when it was determined that there were too many mustangs for the land to support. Callie knew that if she took it upon herself to free these horses, she'd be in major trouble.

Hank entered the corral and the rest of the herd followed. Callie and the vet jumped off the rail before they could be knocked to the ground and trampled by the rampaging horses.

"There must be at least seventy of them!" Callie shouted over the deafening sound of pounding hooves and frantic whinnies. The horses ran from end to end, looking for a way out of the trap. Their eyes rolled white in their heads as they pushed against each other, trying to get as far away as possible from the cowboys and onlookers who lined the fences of the pen.

The horses' coats were slick with sweat and flecked with foam from their long, hard run. Several of the young foals looked ready to drop from exhaustion. One pretty pinto filly slid to the ground when an older mare accidentally knocked into her.

Callie instinctively jumped on the fence, ready to enter the crazed herd to save the foal. Susan grabbed her by the back of her shirt and pointed to the outside rail, where the filly had surfaced with her dam. The foal was dazed and shaking, but seemed to be otherwise unharmed.

Callie thought she saw a pale flash of palomino, but it quickly disappeared into a swirling sea of colors as the wild horses continued to churn up the dirt in the pen. A loud scream drew her attention to the end of the arena, where two stallions had squared off and were preparing to do battle. Even in the middle of total chaos, the brave studs were ready to defend their harems.

After a brief skirmish, the smaller stallion retreated to the other end of the corral and did his best to herd his mares with him.

It seemed an eternity before the horses calmed enough to settle into their own places in the large pen. They stared at each other, their foam-flecked sides heaving and their eyes rolling in terror.

When the dust settled, Susan pointed to a pale shape lying in the middle of the corral. Callie's breath caught in her throat and her heart hammered against her chest. She prayed that the mare lying in the dirt, groaning and gasping for breath, wasn't the horse she had admired so often. But the four white stockings and the sweat-stained blaze on her face told Callie all she needed to know.

Moonbeam had been captured, and she was in big trouble.

Five

rab my bag, Callie!" Susan turned and signaled to the cowboys for help. "We've got a problem. That mare's in labor and she's not looking good."

Callie snatched up the vet's bag and, without thinking, jumped over the fence. She ran toward Moonbeam, desperately wanting to help save the mare. She was halfway to the downed horse when the little mustang raised her head and snorted in fear. Then the horse bolted to her feet and trotted away in a lopsided gait. Callie could hear the veterinarian hollering at her from the gate, but she only had eyes for Moonbeam. The mare stood in the corner with her head lowered, wheezing and groaning.

"Hold on there, Callie!" Sam shouted from the other end of the pen as he moved his horse toward the gate. "Get out of that pen before you start another stampede."

Callie turned to run, but froze in her tracks as a well-muscled bay stallion screamed in challenge and charged toward her. He stopped between Callie and the fence and boldly pawed at the ground, shaking his long, tangled mane and arching his neck.

"Don't move!" Justin called to Callie from atop his horse outside of the pen. "Any movement might make the stallion attack."

Callie gulped. Move? With her heart lodged somewhere in her throat and her blood roaring so loudly she could barely hear the young cowboy's words, she doubted a team of mules could move her. Her feet felt as if they were rooted in the ground like the surrounding sagebrush. She stared into the angry stallion's wild gaze. "Easy, boy…" the words slipped past her lips. "Whoa, son."

The mustang stopped his posturing and pricked his ears, listening intently to the gentle sound. His nostrils extended as he sucked in a giant breath, trying to get the scent of the human who stood before him. He blew hard through his nose, snorting a warning to his mares before lifting his tail over his back and charging in a wide circle around Callie.

She felt a tinge of excitement along with the cold adrenaline rush of fear coursing through her veins. The bay stallion was magnificent! He wheeled around her in a wide arc, his rhythmic hoofbeats pounding a wild tattoo on the dirt floor of the corral. Callie spun in a circle, keeping her eyes focused on the mustang.

"Yaw, yaw!" the cowboys yelled as Sam and Justin entered the pen and rode hard toward the bay stallion. The stud slid to a stop and turned to face the men on horseback, then quickly whirled on his haunches and galloped back to the herd.

"Get back over that fence, young lady!" Sam ordered, then he turned his horse and herded the mustangs to the other end of the large pen. He returned to Callie and swiped his hat from his head, running his shirtsleeve across his sweaty forehead. "You could have been killed!"

Callie bent over the fence, catching her breath. "I'm sorry. I just wanted to help."

The big cowboy softened his voice. "You're a good vet's helper, Callie. You care about the horses." He leaned across the front of his saddle and looked down at her. "But you're not made of steel. If that stallion had decided to charge, you'd be dead right now. If Susan wants a particular horse, she'll call it out and we'll go get it," he said. "That's what Justin and I are here for."

Callie brushed a tangle of hair away from her hot, sticky face as she glanced at Justin. The boy just shook his head and turned away. *Great,* Callie thought. *I've made another good impression.*

Susan peeled her white knuckles from the fence rail and came over to Callie. "Are you okay?" she asked. When Callie nodded, the vet turned to the cowboys and pointed to the herd of mustangs. "I need that yellow mare in the corner. That run was probably too much for her. She's about to foal, and after all that running, it may be turned. We don't want to lose that foal."

Callie gasped. Not Moonbeam's foal! It was bad enough that the mare had been captured and would be put up for adoption, but she couldn't bear the thought of losing the foal, too! She watched as the cowboys closed in and lifted their lassos above their heads. Justin threw his loop first, but it landed on the back of the palomino mare. His father was a better shot. His rope slipped neatly over Moonbeam's head. In the next moment, Justin recovered his lasso and tossed his own rope over the struggling mare's proud head.

Callie watched in horror as the men slowed their horses and

tightened the rope around the mustang's neck, effectively cutting off her wind supply. "Do they have to do it like that?" she asked Susan.

The vet nodded. "I know it seems cruel, but it's the quickest way to isolate the mare." She pushed up her glasses. "Time is of the essence right now. Every minute counts when you've got a foal on the way."

The cowboys pulled the mare into an empty pen and waited for Susan's instructions.

"Let her go and let's see what she does," the vet said.

The cowboys dropped their ropes and exited the corral. They all watched as the mare paced the far wall of the small pen, the two lariats dragging in the sand. Her beautiful head lowered to the ground as she walked. Every now and then she stopped to groan and nip at her sides.

"Is she going to be all right?" Callie asked. She wrung her hands as she watched the little mare drop to the ground and roll, her sweaty coat picking up even more dirt than before. After a minute, the horse rose and began pacing again.

"It's hard to say." Susan rifled through her medical bag and pulled out a bottle of tranquilizer and a syringe. "From the looks of her milk bag, I'd say she was probably a week or two away from being ready to foal before this roundup."

Callie bit her bottom lip, secretly wishing she had thrown a rock or two at that stupid helicopter. Moonbeam and her unborn foal *had* to be all right! She looked to Susan, afraid to voice the question for fear that her trembling words would give away how scared she was.

The vet lifted the syringe to the waning light and flicked it with her thumb and forefinger, dispelling any air bubbles. She gave Callie an encouraging smile. "The mare should be okay, as long as there aren't any complications."

"What's going on here?" Harvey Smith shuffled up to the pen, moving as fast as his bowed legs and walking stick would carry him. "I could hear all the hollering going on from the office. What are you so excited about?"

"Some new mustangs have been brought in," Callie said. She peeked through the fence. Moonbeam's knees buckled as she lowered herself to the ground and stretched fully onto her side. "This mare's ready to foal, but Susan thinks it's too soon." Callie shook her head. "I've followed this mustang for a couple of years. She's my favorite. If she makes it through this, I'd like to adopt her. I'll need to find a way to earn some extra money, though, and then I'll have to talk my parents into it."

The veterinarian smiled. "Maybe we'll get lucky and you'll have a two-in-one package." She turned to the Sam and Justin. "Do you think we can get her into the squeeze chute to give her a tranquilizer?"

Justin ducked through the fence. Moonbeam eyed him warily, but stayed where she was, her sides heaving as she quivered in pain. She moved to a more upright position with her legs tucked under and turned her head to nip at her flanks before lying back in the dirt again.

"I don't think that cayuse is going anywhere." The gruff, nasally voice came from Ron Jeffers, the head man at the mustang pens. He walked up and stood beside Harvey and Callie, his thin frame towering over them. "If she doesn't make it, get the tractor and haul her around back." He flipped a knowing look to Susan. "You know the routine." He gave them all a dismissing nod as he walked away.

Callie frowned at the slang term Mr. Jeffers had used to refer to Moonbeam. Cayuse was the word people used to show how little they thought of mustangs. As far as she was concerned, this mustang was worth more than Mr. Jeffers.

Harvey put a comforting arm around Callie's shoulders. "Don't pay him any mind," he advised. "Right now we've got to think about that little mare out there, and how to help her."

Sam got off his horse and walked toward the exhausted mare. "One of the other men and I can hold her head down while you get the needle into her neck," he volunteered. He gestured to a large man who had helped bring in the herd. "No mustang's going to die on my shift," he muttered, casting an angry glare in the direction of the boss.

Susan looked doubtful. "I guess it's our only choice," she said. "Callie, you run up to the house and get me two buckets of warm water. Put some Betadine in both and be quick about it."

Callie took one last look at the suffering mare, then turned and ran as fast as she could toward the ranch house. She knew it was only a matter of minutes, but it seemed like an eternity before the buckets were full and she was sloshing her way back to the pens. She set the pails down next to the vet. "How is she?"

Susan shook her head. "It doesn't look good. Her water broke, but we don't have any front feet showing yet. It's possible that the baby hasn't turned completely, or was jostled into a bad position during the capture."

Callie set her jaw and stared at the waning sun. The calm beauty of the desert belied the struggle that was going on here at the corral.

"Okay, here we go," Susan said. Everyone gathered around the outside of the pen to watch. After what seemed like an extremely long wait, two tiny black hooves emerged from the mare.

Callie smiled and breathed a little easier. Everything was going to be all right.

They waited for the nose to appear on the next labored push from Moonbeam, but nothing happened. After several more attempts to expel the foal from her body, the mustang groaned and closed her eyes, breathing in quick, shallow grunts.

"Something's definitely wrong." Susan pulled on her latex gloves. "Men, I need you to hold the mare again. I think the foal's head is out of position. I'm going to have to go in and realign it."

Callie planted her hands on her knees and bent down to watch the vet work. The sight of blood made her woozy, but her fear for the mare and foal outweighed the dizziness and the tiny white dots that danced before her eyes. She held her breath and wondered if anyone could see how scared she was. She glanced up at Harvey, hoping for some sign of encouragement, but he looked nervous, too.

Callie wiped at the sweat that covered her face despite the cool evening breeze. She felt old Harvey's gnarled hand on her shoulder and smiled her thanks.

The vet worked quickly, trying to reposition the foal. Moonbeam groaned and struggled against the men, but their body weight kept her head pinned to the ground. After another painful wheeze, the mare submitted to human help.

"I've got it!" Susan manipulated the foal, carefully guiding it into position.

Callie fought the wave of blackness that threatened to pull her into its depths. She breathed deeply, huffing along with Moonbeam as the mare groaned and stiffened her legs with the next contraction. Harvey braced one of his scarecrow-thin arms around Callie's shoulders, and she leaned against the frail old man, hoping that her little bit of weight wouldn't be enough to knock him over.

"Here we go," Susan said as Moonbeam gave a mighty push.

Callie wanted to jump and shout when a tiny pink nose appeared between the small black hooves. She felt tears gathering in her eyes. With the next push, the foal's neck and shoulders appeared. Moonbeam rested for a moment, then began the final push.

"Come on, you can do it," Callie whispered, sharing a small smile with Justin from across the pen. He seemed a lot nicer when he smiled, she thought.

As they looked on, the little foal's nostrils, which had been pinched closed for the birthing process, spasmed open, gathering a first breath even before the foal was completely free from its mother's body.

Callie forgot about fainting. She leaned closer, wanting to place an encouraging hand on Moonbeam's coat, but she knew better than to touch the wild mare. For now she'd have to be content to lend moral support.

The palomino grunted again and strained to relieve her body of the foal. The new baby slipped into the world, eyeing Callie and the veterinarian as it lay in the dirt, attempting to raise its delicate head.

Goose bumps galloped up and down Callie's arms. "He's perfect," she whispered in awe as she stared at the buckskin foal.

The colt had the exact shade of pale yellow coat as Moonbeam, but its mane and tail were black like its sire's.

"She," Susan corrected. "It's a filly. Hand me the iodine, then grab a clean cloth. I'll take care of the umbilical cord while you clean out her nostrils. We've got to work quickly. I want to have this filly checked out before her mama gets up."

Callie crouched in the dirt beside the still-wet foal. The metallic scent of blood mixed with amniotic fluid and the drying sweat of the exhausted mare assaulted her nose and caused her stomach to roll. She tried to ignore the waves of nausea and concentrated on the light perfume of desert peach that drifted on the evening air. "Shouldn't she be standing and trying to nurse?"

"Give her time," the vet offered as she put a stethoscope to the newborn's chest. "She's a pretty weak little girl. She needs to gather all her energy first. If she hasn't eaten in two hours, we can start to worry."

"She's darned near perfect." Old Harvey beamed.

Justin stepped forward, handing Callie a towel from the vet's bag. "Thanks," she said.

It was almost dark now, but there was enough light to work by. The sound of a night bird echoed down the mountain. It was soon answered by its mate. Callie smiled and folded the cloth around her index finger, moving her hand toward the foal's nose. The filly lifted her head and made sucking noises, her little pink tongue curling upward in search of nourishment.

"Look!" Callie exclaimed. "She's ready to eat right now."

"We have a few things to get done first." Susan rolled the foal onto its side and quickly doctored the navel cord. "I don't like messing too much with a mustang foal, but night's falling fast, and this filly isn't as strong as she should be. We need to get her dried off. Take that towel and gently wipe her coat down."

Callie rubbed the fluffy towel over the trembling filly, marveling at her wispy black mane that contrasted so sharply with the rest of her light-colored body. "I think I'll call her Moon Shadow." Callie toweled the foal's ears and laughed as the filly shook her finely chiseled head. "She's pale as a moonbeam, like her mother, but she's got this dark, shadowy mane and tail like her sire. Besides, look at that." Callie pointed to the horizon.

Darkness had fallen, and the soft light of the full moon crested over the black outline of the mountains. "She was born in the shadow of the moon," Callie explained.

Susan smiled. "It's a good name. Let's hope she gets a chance to use it. Climb back over the fence. We'll leave the two of them alone for a while and see if nature takes its course."

Everyone stood outside the pen, waiting for the mare to get to her feet so she could encourage her foal to stand and nurse. When Moonbeam continued to lie on her side, one of the cowboys went in to rouse her. The mare staggered to her feet, swaying as her knees threatened to buckle again.

The newborn foal whinnied in concern at the sudden movement, but she continued to lie in the soft dirt of the corral. The weakened mare nickered to her foal and pushed her gently with her muzzle, encouraging her to rise.

Moon Shadow stretched her spindly legs in front of her and bounded to her feet, wobbling like a pinion pine in a strong wind. Another nudge from her dam sent the filly sprawling to the dirt, where she squealed and tried to rise again. After her third attempt, Moon Shadow rose and slowly shuffled to her mother in search of milk.

"That's a good sign," Susan said. "I had my doubts about whether she was going to have the strength to do that. If she can nurse, she'll get stronger with each passing meal." The vet zipped her bag closed. "That's it. Let's pack it in. Thanks for the help, everyone. I'll stop by in the morning to see how things are going."

Callie didn't want to leave the horses, but she knew her mother and father were waiting at home, holding up their dinner until she got there. With one last look at Moonbeam and her foal, Callie slipped over the fence and headed for Susan's pickup. She and Susan had just buckled themselves in when the sound of boot heels on hard-packed dirt echoed up the driveway. It was Justin.

"Doc, wait, don't leave yet!" He pulled his Stetson from his head and nervously turned it over and over in his hands. "Something's wrong with the palomino mare. She's down in the dirt again, rolling from side to side. You'd better come quick!"

Six

❦

Callie jumped out of the truck and flew toward the mustang pens. Moonbeam needed her! Callie was the first one over the fence, and her feet hit the dirt with such force that she almost tumbled to the ground. Luckily there were no other mustangs in the small pen to worry about. As she recovered her balance, the groans of the troubled mare reached her ears. Callie moved as close to the pale yellow mare as she dared.

The foal she had named Moon Shadow teetered on shaky legs, nickering in alarm as her dam rolled to her other side, her legs beating a rhythm on the dusty earth. Moonbeam sensed she wasn't alone and lifted her head, rolling her eyes in fear.

"What's wrong with her?" Callie asked Susan anxiously as the vet entered the pen, followed by Sam and Justin. She fought the urge to move closer to the mare. The way Moonbeam was thrashing about, anyone within three feet of her would risk a broken leg, or worse. She watched in horror as the newborn filly tried to get close to her mother, and was sent sprawling into the dirt as the mare renewed her struggles.

"Somebody do something!" Callie screamed. Heedless of the

sharp hooves, she ran toward the newborn filly, sliding to the ground beside her tiny body. She tasted the chalky earth as she wrapped her arms around the foal.

"Callie, no!" Sam and Susan hollered in unison as they ran to help.

The mare whinnied in alarm and began to thrash about. Callie felt a sharp sting as Moonbeam's hoof scraped across her arm. She sucked in her breath and bit her bottom lip to keep from crying out. The foal moved weakly within her grasp, tossing her head and flailing her legs in an attempt to free herself.

"Justin, you help Callie while we try to find out what's the matter with this mare," Sam said.

Callie yelped as Moon Shadow's head connected with her cheekbone. The sharp *crack* echoed across the corral so loudly, she wondered if she'd broken something. Ignoring the pain, she pulled the filly closer to her body and rolled her out of harm's way.

Moon Shadow whinnied in protest, lunging against the arms that restrained her.

"Hold her tight, Callie," Justin said as he stepped in to help.

Susan opened her medical bag and took out a bottle. "We've got to get this mare sedated before she really hurts herself."

The desperate mare flopped on the ground, banging her head on the earth of the corral. A second later, Moonbeam groaned and all four of her legs went stiff at once, as if she were having a seizure. Callie tightened her hold on the foal, ignoring the animal's squeal of complaint.

Justin put his arms around Callie and the foal, edging them

over to the corner. "Let's get out of the way so her momma doesn't hurt you or her baby," he said, glancing over his shoulder at the sick mustang.

The vet took advantage of Moonbeam's temporary stillness and moved in to deliver a shot of tranquilizer while Sam held her head. Within moments, the quivering mustang seemed to relax and she lay on her side, breathing heavily. The pale light from the full moon reflected off the white blaze on her face.

Callie could make out the rise and fall of the mare's rib cage as her labored breaths disturbed the momentary silence. "Is she going to be all right?"

Her words were only a whisper, but they boomed across the sudden quiet, startling the foal in her arms and causing her to renew her struggles. Callie buried her face in Moon Shadow's neck and held on tight until she grew still once more.

Callie said a silent prayer as she watched Susan move her stethoscope across the mare's belly, listening intently. When the vet turned, Callie could tell by her expression that things weren't good.

The vet tugged the stethoscope from around her neck and shook her head. "This mare's got a twisted gut. It probably happened on the run here, or when she lay down to foal." She placed a sympathetic hand on the sedated mustang. "I'm not hearing any gut sounds. If this were just a colic, there would be plenty of noise in her belly. I think it's too late to save her. I'm going to have to put her down before it gets worse."

"No!" Callie tried to shout, but the word fell from her lips like the last wilted leaf on a winter tree.

This couldn't be happening. Not to Moonbeam! She was a young mare. And now, she had a foal to take care of. What would become of Moon Shadow if her mother was gone? Callie's head swam with jumbled thoughts. She hugged the newborn foal closer to her chest. "There's got to be something we can do!" she cried. "Moon Shadow needs her mother. How will she survive without her?"

The vet sighed. "If we put the mare down, we could be condemning the filly to the same fate. But we've got no other choice. This mustang has a twisted intestine. She's already in unbearable pain. If we just let her go, she'll die a slow, agonizing death. I can't let that happen."

Callie stared through the moonlit night at the little mare that just a few short days ago had been full of promise and life. Now, with her coat saturated with sweat and dirt and her body wracked with pain, she bore no resemblance to the proud mustang mare that had raced over the desert hills.

Moonbeam groaned and Callie tried her best to keep from crying. She knew Susan was right. The longer they waited, the harder it would be on the horse. Her eyes met Justin's. He twisted his hat in his hands and looked away.

Susan left the corral and headed for her truck. Callie knew she'd return with two syringes full of tranquilizer. The sedative would be painless, quick acting, and deadly when given in a large dose.

The foal stirred in Callie's arms, whickering softly to her dam. Callie tried to swallow the lump in her throat, but it wouldn't go down. There were so many questions she wanted to ask, but the pressure building behind her eyes and the back of her throat warned her that speaking might break loose the sobs that waited to burst from her chest.

She swallowed hard. "Will Moon Shadow die, too?" she asked, looking directly into Sam's face. He'd worked with horses for many years and had seen it all. He'd know the score.

Sam pulled the hat from his head, slapped it against his dusty chaps, and stared into the star-filled sky.

"I don't rightly know the full answer to that one, Callie," Sam said, working his fingers around the stiff brim of his hat. "I've seen an orphaned foal foster onto another mare that lost her own colt, and that foal ended up just fine and dandy. I've even bottle-fed a few and pulled them through the worst of times. But I'll be honest with you. I've also seen a lot of them die."

Callie watched the man plunk his hat back onto his head and set his mouth in a firm line. He'd said his fill. She knew she'd get nothing further from him. She'd have to cling to those flimsy rays of hope.

When Susan returned, Callie asked, "Will it work? Can we foster Moon Shadow onto another mare?"

Susan rubbed her eyes. "That depends on whether we can find another mare who's nursing a foal. Most of the time they won't take another one, though. The best answer would be to find a mare that's lost her own baby and is willing to take care of another mare's foal."

Callie searched her memory, trying to remember how many mares and foals had been driven in that day.

"Better turn that filly over to Justin," Sam said, nodding toward his son. "She may struggle pretty hard when we put her momma down."

Callie clung to the filly a moment longer, closing her eyes and pressing her face into the soft hair on Moon Shadow's neck. She breathed in the warm horse scent while hot tears streamed down the side of her face.

Justin tapped her on the shoulder. Callie tightened her grip on the filly.

"I won't let anything happen to her," Justin reassured her. He knelt in the dirt and put his arms around the tiny foal.

Callie reluctantly gave way to the young cowboy's firm grip on the mustang.

"Hold these for me, Callie," Susan requested. She handed two syringes to Callie before turning to stroke the mare's neck, looking for the artery.

Callie pursed her lips as she stared at the tranquilizer she held in her hands. It was too dark to see, but she knew the liquid in the shots was pink. She had watched Susan put down other horses. But this time it was different. This time Callie felt a personal connection to the horse.

Callie gripped the syringes. She considered throwing them as hard as she could into the sagebrush, but a loud groan from Moonbeam brought her back to her senses. The mare was in unbearable pain. It would only get worse if they waited.

"We're ready," Susan said as she motioned for the first shot.

Callie stepped forward and handed her the syringe. When the vet administered the first dose, Moonbeam began a series of long, deep breaths.

As she watched the mustang mare, Callie's head begin to spin and the ground tilted under her shoes. She wanted to run, to hide from this awful ordeal, but her feet remained rooted to the spot.

Susan injected the final, fatal dose of the sedative. Moonbeam drew several more ragged breaths, then she released one long, breathy sigh and lay still.

Callie felt the world slip away beneath her. She cried out as she hit the ground, her palms scraping against the rough earth. A moment later, strong hands gently clutched her arms, helping her to her feet. She lifted her tear-drenched eyes to stare into Justin's concerned face.

"Take her over to my truck," Susan said. "I'll be there in a moment to take her home."

Justin pulled Callie by the hand, leading her back to the truck. She glanced back at Moonbeam as she stumbled along after him. The palomino mare lay still in the moonlight. Moon Shadow walked around her mother in confusion, nickering and poking her dam with her soft nose.

The sight tore at Callie's heart and a wall of tears came flooding loose. She tried to hold back her sobs, but she couldn't stop them. She almost tripped over a rock, and Justin held onto her arm to keep her upright. Callie winced and dug her heels into the dirt, forcing him to stop. She knew it wasn't fair, but the pain tearing at her heart made her want to take her frustrations out on somebody, and he was the closest.

"Let me go!" Callie cried, pulling her arm from Justin's grasp.

He let go and stepped back, looking at her like she was a snake ready to strike. "I was only trying to help."

"I don't need your help!" Callie screamed between choking gasps of breath. "Just go back to the pen with your dad. You've got a dead horse to bury!" She saw the hurt look on the boy's face and felt even worse. She covered her mouth to keep more sobs from escaping, then turned and ran the rest of the way to the truck.

Callie climbed into the little white pickup and dragged her sleeve across her wet eyes. When her vision cleared, she could see that Justin was still standing in the same spot, watching her. She crossed her arms and stared defiantly at him through the windshield. He probably thought she was the biggest baby he'd ever seen.

The long-legged boy walked slowly to the pickup and stared in the window. "I'll take care of your filly, Callie," he promised. "I won't let anything happen to her."

Callie watched as Justin spun on his boot heels and walked off with his hands jammed in his pockets. She felt like a bigger jerk than ever. He was only trying to be nice to her, and she'd turned on him like a rabid dog. She'd gotten off on the wrong foot with him from the start. After the way she had just behaved, she doubted the young cowboy would ever forgive her. But worse than that, Moonbeam was gone.

She put her head in her hands and sobbed.

Seven

✦

Callie stared out the truck's window at the full moon. She wiped her eyes with a tissue and took a few steadying breaths. It was time to stop crying now. Crying wouldn't help Moonbeam or her orphaned foal.

Susan opened the door of the truck and climbed in.

"How's Moon Shadow?" Callie asked, fumbling with the torn edge of her shirt.

The vet turned the key in the ignition and the engine roared to life. "There was some mare's milk with colostrum stored at the office. We got a good dose of that down her with a feeding tube. I sedated her a little and left the tube in so the cowboys can feed her a couple more times during the night. In the morning, Sam wants to try putting Moon Shadow in with another mare and foal to see if the mare will take her. If not, we'll have to try bottle-feeding her." Susan glanced at Callie as she put the truck in gear and backed out of their spot. "If she won't take the bottle, she probably won't make it."

Callie leaned her head against the side window and stared at the shadowy desert that lay under the light of the moon. She'd lost Moonbeam forever. The beautiful mustang would never again gallop over this sage-covered land. She refused to lose the filly, too. She hoped the mare would accept the newborn foal. If not, then she planned to do everything she could to get Moon Shadow to take a bottle.

Clamping her lips together in determination, Callie looked back toward the mustang pens. Somehow, she'd find a way to save Moon Shadow.

"I called your folks and told them what was happening," Susan said as she turned onto the road that led to Callie's house. "Your mom has your dinner warming on the stove."

Callie wrinkled her nose. Dinner was the last thing she wanted right now. "Are you going back to the pens tonight to check on Moon Shadow?" she asked.

Susan shook her head. "Sam assured me that he's done this kind of thing a hundred times," she told Callie. "He'll feed the little filly during the night, and I'll be there first thing in the morning. He has my cell number if he needs me."

Seeing that Callie was about to protest, Susan held up her hand. "Moon Shadow will be fine," the vet said. "You need to get a good night's sleep so you'll have a clear head in the morning." She slowed the truck down and turned into Callie's driveway.

Callie thanked Susan for the ride and made arrangements to meet her the next morning. Then she turned and walked toward the house. Her mother met her at the door with a big hug.

"I'm sorry to hear about that mustang, honey," she said. "I know how much that little mare meant to you. Susan tells me that her filly is still alive."

Callie nodded as she extricated herself from her mother's bear hug and bent to take off her shoes. "I'm really tired, Mom. Is it okay if I skip dinner and go straight to bed? I've got to be up early to meet Susan in the morning."

Her mother started to insist, then gave in to Callie's pleading look. "Okay," Mrs. McLean said. "I don't suppose you have much of an appetite now anyway. I'll make you a good breakfast tomorrow." She kissed Callie on the top of her head and shooed her toward her bedroom.

❧

Callie washed her face and brushed her teeth, then crawled into bed and pulled the covers up to her chin. She closed her eyes, but sleep was hard to find. When the alarm finally went off in the morning, her covers were on the floor. With all the tossing and turning, Callie doubted she had slept more than two hours total.

Reaching over to turn off the alarm clock, Callie squinted at the first rays of dawn spilling through the gap in her hand-stitched curtains. She slid her legs over the side of the bed and quickly pulled on her jeans and a T-shirt, then padded down the hallway.

Mrs. McLean smiled when Callie entered the kitchen. "I made your favorite breakfast: oatmeal with cinnamon toast and a big glass of orange juice."

Callie shook her head and reached for her boots. "I'm not very hungry. I'll just wait outside for Susan."

"Have a seat," her mother said firmly as she pulled out a chair. "Susan called about ten minutes ago. She had an emergency to attend to on the other side of town and won't be out to the pens for at least an hour or two. She said to tell you that the filly made it through the night."

Callie heaved a sigh of relief and sat down to breakfast. She still didn't have much of an appetite, but she knew her mother wouldn't let her out of the house without eating something. She stuffed a big bite of toast into her mouth and chewed quickly. She had to get to Moon Shadow as soon as possible. "Can you give me a ride to the pens this morning?" she asked as she reached for the glass of orange juice.

"Your father's already taken the car into town to deliver some fresh lettuce and asparagus to the local stores."

Callie couldn't hide her disappointment.

"Why don't you take Celah?" Mrs. McLean suggested. "The pens aren't that far away. The tractor's still broken, but your father won't need the mare until later today. I'll drop him by the pens after lunch so he can bring her home. You can catch a ride with Susan when you're finished."

"Thanks, Mom." Callie rose from her chair. "I'll go get Celah ready right now."

"Just a minute, young lady," her mother said as she pointed to the untouched bowl of oatmeal. "You're not going anywhere until you've eaten a few more bites."

"Mom!" Callie complained as she sat back down and stirred the bowl of cooked oats. "I really need to see how Moon Shadow is doing." She gulped a couple of spoonfuls of the hot cereal, hoping it would be enough to satisfy her mother.

"Moon Shadow?" Mrs. McLean's eyebrows rose. "You didn't tell us you'd named the little mustang."

Callie looked down at her oatmeal. By the time she'd come home last night, she'd been too upset to think. She'd forgotten to mention a lot of things—like her plans to adopt Moon Shadow if the foal survived.

She knew her parents wouldn't be happy about that idea. The mustang would be an *unnecessary frivolity*, as her father called anything they couldn't sell or that didn't earn its keep.

Callie frowned. Did everything on the farm have to have some big purpose? They raised their own beef cows, grew their own vegetables—which Callie helped her mother can every fall. To pay for things they couldn't grow, her parents sold the vegetables and herbs from their garden.

"Look, honey," her mother said as she ran a caring hand over Callie's hair. "I know how much it hurt you to lose that palomino mustang. Maybe it's not such a good idea to get attached to her foal."

Callie tapped her spoon against the bowl. This definitely wasn't the right time to mention adopting Moon Shadow. She couldn't bear the thought of her parents saying no. She had to figure out a way to bring the filly home. She might be Moon Shadow's only hope.

Callie slugged down the rest of the oatmeal and finished off the glass of juice. "Can I go now?" She scooted out of the chair before her mother had a chance to answer.

"Here, take this," Mrs. McLean said as she handed her an apple. "And make sure that you get a couple bites of it before you feed it to Celah."

"Thanks, Mom. You're the best." Callie grabbed the apple and headed for the door. "I'll see you later," she hollered as the screen door banged shut behind her. She hurried to Celah's pen and whistled for the big black. The mare lifted her head from the hay pile, turned toward Callie and flicked her ears, then went back to eating.

"Oh, no you don't," Callie said as she grabbed the lead rope from the fence. "You'll be dining on government hay today. You can eat when we get to the mustang pens." She slipped over the fence and snapped the rope onto Celah's halter, pulling several times before she persuaded the big mare to go with her.

She tied the draft horse to the hitching post outside the old barn, offering her a handful of sweet feed to make up for the early ending to her breakfast. She quickly brushed and bridled the mare, then coaxed her over to the nearest barrel and hopped onto her broad back. When they reached the sand trail that led to the back of the mustang corrals, she prodded Celah into a trot.

Twenty minutes later, Callie halted the big horse on the ridge overlooking the corrals. She squinted into the early morning sun and noticed movement in the center pen below. Shielding her eyes with her hand, she made out Justin's black Stetson. A flash of jealousy stabbed through her chest when she saw that he was handling Moon Shadow. With Moonbeam gone, Callie knew that the little buckskin filly would imprint on those closest to her in her first few days. And she wanted it to be her!

She pressed her heels into Celah's sides and guided her down the gentle slope to the back of the pens.

Justin's head snapped around as Callie and Celah came

nearer. It was hard to miss the echo of the two-thousand-pound horse's huge feet as she plodded down the trail.

The boy straightened and waved her over to the pen where Moon Shadow was teetering around on unsteady legs. "Come see your filly," he said. "We got a couple more meals into her during the night. My dad just pulled the feeding tube. He wants to try fostering her onto this other mare as soon as the vet gets here."

Your filly, Justin had said. Callie felt a pang of regret at her jealous thoughts just a moment ago.

Justin tucked his thumbs into his belt loops and watched Callie and Celah approach. "That's an awfully big horse for such a little girl," he said.

The words "little girl" hung in the air. Callie frowned at him and swung her legs over the mare's side, dropping to the ground with a bone-jarring *thump*. "I can handle her," she said, in a more snappish tone than she had intended. Her lack of sleep was making her touchy. She opened the gate of an empty pen and stood on her toes to remove Celah's bridle, then grabbed a flake of hay from a nearby pile and tossed it in the feeder.

Justin pulled his Stetson down on his forehead and grinned. "I'm sure you can." He looked over the big mare. "I've never been on a horse that large. Maybe you'll let me ride her sometime?"

Callie glanced over her shoulder to see if the young cowboy was kidding. Her rotten neighbor, Luke, was forever teasing her about the draft mare. Justin's sleek paint would rival any of the horses on Luke's ranch. Maybe he had the same stuck-up opinion of Celah.

She noted the open smile on Justin's face and decided that he might not be making fun of her after all. "Sure," she said. "If you're not worried about falling off."

Justin laughed. "Don't worry. When I've got that far to fall, I'll be extra careful."

Callie studied the young cowboy again. He seemed sincere. Maybe he was just trying to make up for the bad start. He was definitely trying to help save Moon Shadow, so he couldn't be *that* bad.

"The last time I fell off Celah, I couldn't sit down for a week."

"I bet." He motioned her into the corral. "Come see your filly."

Callie followed him, smiling to herself. He'd said Moon Shadow had been fed a couple times during the night. That meant there was hope. She entered the pen where Moon Shadow wobbled around on her long, spindly legs. "She doesn't look like she's improved much," Callie said in concern as she took in the filly's gaunt sides and weak appearance.

"Well, I wouldn't exactly say that she's thriving," Justin said, walking up to the skittish filly. He crooned soft words to her as he extended his hand to touch the foal's golden coat. "But at least she's still alive."

Callie felt another wrench of jealousy when Moon Shadow gave a soft nicker to the boy.

"She's improved a little," he added. He wrapped his arms around Moon Shadow to stop her from running away and motioned with a nod of his head. "Come touch her. She's really soft."

Callie stepped forward slowly, extending her hand toward the filly's neck. She knew that the center of a horse's forehead was like a blind spot. Patting a wild horse there might cause it to react in fright. Horses were prey animals. In the wild, they were the hunted instead of the hunter. They needed vision that enabled them to see forward, to the sides, and behind them; that's why their eyes were on the sides of their head. Callie softly stroked the filly's neck, then trailed her hands up toward the filly's cheekbones.

"You're good with horses," Justin observed with an approving smile.

Callie felt herself blush at the unexpected compliment. "I want to be an equine vet like Susan someday," she told him. She ran her fingers through the filly's wispy, black mane, marveling at its soft, silky feel. "Then I can help save horses like she does."

"My dad put that foster mare and her foal into the pen next to Moon Shadow this morning to see if the mare showed any interest," Justin said. He let Moon Shadow go, chuckling as she ambled away on unsteady legs. "But the mare just kept pinning her ears at her and kicking the fence every time she got close. We've got another mare that lost her foal and still has milk. We're hoping she'll want to take on Moon Shadow in place of her own foal. We ran her into that corral a couple of pens away just before you got here."

Callie stared over the fence at the plain brown mare. Her mane was tangled and her tail almost touched the ground. She didn't look like much, but she represented hope for Moon Shadow.

"My dad rubbed some fresh mint into the mare's nostrils," Justin said.

"Why'd he do that?" Callie asked. She'd never heard of such a thing.

"Mares recognize the scent of their foal," he explained. "If it smells different, they reject the baby. Putting the mint in her nostrils might help block the smell. Hopefully, she'll accept Moon Shadow." Justin furrowed his brow. "Orphans do a lot better on fresh mare's milk than they do on the powdered stuff you buy in the store. With Moon Shadow being so weak and all, we really need this other mare to take her on."

Callie heard the worry in Justin's voice. She tried not to panic, but another look at the struggling mustang foal told her that everything he said was true. "But what about the tube feeding she got through the night?" Callie asked. "Didn't that help?"

Justin nodded. "It gave her a good start. She needed to get that first milk down her. That's what helps her build the antibodies she'll need to survive. But tube-feeding is no way for this filly to grow up. My dad says it should only be used for medical emergencies. She needs to nurse from a mare. That's her best shot. If that doesn't work, then she'll have to learn to drink store-bought powdered foal milk from a bottle, or maybe you can find a milk goat."

"I can bottle-feed her," Callie was quick to volunteer.

Justin studied her from beneath the broad brim of his Stetson. "You ever bottle-fed a foal before?"

Callie hung her head, giving a brief shake to show that she had no such experience.

"Well, it's no picnic," Justin cautioned. "I've done it before and it's a lot of work. You have to feed around the clock every couple of hours for the first few weeks. And since it won't be her momma's milk, the milk substitute will cause problems of its own. You'll have to watch that she doesn't get the scours, or colic. Either of those could kill her. Are you sure you want to handle all of that?"

Callie crossed her arms. "Of course I do. I'd do anything to help Moon Shadow!"

Justin cocked his head, giving her a funny look. "Yeah? Why would you go to all that trouble? It's not like it's *your* horse or anything. You'll do all of that work, and if she lives, then somebody else will adopt her."

"Well, she could be mine," Callie said stubbornly. "If my mom and dad will let me adopt her."

Justin shook his head. "My dad says it costs the same to feed a mustang as it does a registered horse. In fact, this filly will probably cost you more, because she's going to need a lot of vet work to keep her healthy. And after you pour all that money into her, she'll still be just a mutt horse."

Callie scowled. How could she have ever thought she might be friends with this boy? "Moon Shadow's not just a mutt horse!" she said hotly. "A mustang can do anything your fancy registered horse can do! They're tough. Not like some of those prissy show horses," she added.

Justin held up his hands to ward off Callie's attack. "Hey, hold on just a second. I didn't say she was worthless. I just mean that she's going to take a lot of work. *If* she lives. Horses that are sickly early in their lives sometimes have problems later. Let's hope it doesn't come to that, but it could."

Justin turned his head at the sound of metal clanging on metal. "That's Dr. Susan and my dad." He pointed to the front gate where Sam and the vet were stepping through. "Let's go make sure the foster mare is ready."

Callie followed Justin over to the surrogate mare's pen. This mare was Moon Shadow's best bet for a healthy life. She crossed her fingers, hoping that their plan would work.

Eight

꧁✿꧂

G ood morning, Callie." Sam Rosser tipped his hat and smiled. "You're here awfully early after the late night we had last night."

"She's moonin' over that sad little mustang filly," Justin teased, pushing his hat back with his thumb.

Callie wanted to sock him a good one. Justin seemed almost as bad as Luke. Why did boys always like to tease?

"Now, don't be knocking those mustangs, son," Sam advised as he opened the gate to let Susan into the brown mare's pen. "Some of the cowboys here are riding former wild horses, and they're pretty good mounts." He winked at Callie. "Those mustangs off the Elko range have a lot of good blood in them from the times when ranchers turned out their registered mounts to help improve the herds."

Callie smiled gratefully at Sam. "The mustang is my favorite kind of horse," she admitted. "Someday I'm going to own one." She jammed her hands into the pockets of her jeans and scuffed the dirt with the toe of her boot.

Sam looked over his shoulder at Callie. "Are you maybe

thinking that yellow filly with the black points might be the one for you?"

Callie nodded. "If I can talk my parents into it."

Justin's dad ran his fingers over his salt-and-pepper mustache. "Then I guess we'd better make sure she survives this ordeal. Let's go get her and see if our experiment is going to work."

Callie felt the grin spread across her face. At least *somebody* was on her side. She took big steps, trying to match the older cowboy's long-legged stride as they went to get Moon Shadow.

Justin held the gate while his father cornered the filly. Moon Shadow was so small that Sam picked her up in his arms and carried her over to the pen next to the brown mare.

Susan herded Moon Shadow into the upper corner of the enclosure. "We'll introduce them first with a fence between them," she explained. "If the mare seems accepting of her, we'll put them together in the same pen. If she shows aggressive behavior, then we're all out of options for a natural upbringing of this filly."

Sam stared thoughtfully at the small brown horse that they hoped would play nursemaid to the new orphan. "Her bag is heavy with milk, but there was no evidence of a colt at her side when she came in," he said. "I'm hoping she misses her own baby so much that she's willing to take on this one. I figure we've got the next twenty-four hours to turn this filly around. If Moon Shadow isn't nursing on her own or bottle-feeding by tomorrow morning, I don't think we can save her."

Callie's breath caught in her throat. She knew Sam had done this enough times to know what he was talking about. And he had just made the same prediction that Susan had made the night before. "If this doesn't work, *I'll* bottle-feed her," Callie said.

Justin propped a booted foot on the fence. "I already warned her how much trouble that'll be," he told his father. "But I can tell by the stubborn look on her face, she'll do it."

Sam turned to Callie. "You've lived around here for a long time. Why this particular mustang?" he asked. "You must've seen thousands of them come through this facility."

Callie blinked back the tears, thinking about Moon Shadow's dam. She locked eyes with the older cowboy, then looked away, afraid that he might see the fear in her face. "I used to follow Moon Shadow's mother," Callie admitted. "She roamed the hills behind my house for years. I always dreamed that one day I might ride her." She stared off at the distant hills and took several steadying breaths. "Now she's dead, and Moon Shadow doesn't have anyone but me to care about her."

Sam put a large callused hand on Callie's shoulder. "I'm going to do everything I can to save that filly for you, young lady."

Callie smiled at him gratefully.

"Me, too." Justin reassured her. "I'm sorry I teased you, Callie, but I didn't mean any harm. If that mustang's so important to you, my pa and I will do what we can to save her."

Susan nudged Moon Shadow out of the corner. "Well, if everyone's ready, let's see what happens."

Callie held her breath as they introduced the bay mare and Moon Shadow through the fence.

The bay nickered to the filly and poked her nose through the fence, sniffing curiously. Moon Shadow shuffled forward on spindly legs and made sucking noises to the older horse.

Callie jumped when the mustang mare suddenly squealed and struck out with a foreleg, and then extended her nose through the fence once more to nuzzle the foal. "What was that?" she asked as she watched Moon Shadow maneuver toward the mare's flank.

"What's going on out here?" Old Harvey slowly made his way over to the fence. "Everyone's having a party, and no one invited me?" he said with a wink at Callie. He pointed his cane toward the mustang mare. "That's just mare talk, young'un. That's what they do when they're excited or displeased with something," he explained. "Don't let it bother you."

Callie frowned. "If she doesn't like Moon Shadow, I don't think we should put them in together."

Sam crossed to the gate that separated the two horses. "This mare doesn't seem to want to hurt the filly none. She's just making a lot of noise. That's common with these mares and foals." He motioned to his son. "Justin, why don't you step in here with your rope while I let this mare into the pen? If there's any trouble, make a lot of racket and rattle that rope. We'll chase her back out again." He nodded to Callie. "Once the mare's in here, I want you to work the gate. We might have to move her out in a hurry. Can you do that?"

Callie swallowed hard and nodded. She was terrified for Moon Shadow. Although the bay was a small horse, she was still ten times bigger than the foal. So many things could go wrong. But Callie reminded herself again that this wasn't the first time the cowboys had done this. It had worked in the past. It could work for Moon Shadow, too. It was their best hope. They should at least give it a try.

She quickly climbed the fence and went to her post. Justin stood ready while his father opened the gate. The mare immediately trotted into the pen, arching her neck as she approached the foal. She stopped several yards from Moon Shadow and stuck out her nose. The filly softly nickered and took several teetering steps toward the mare, but the mustang pinned her ears and snorted.

"Easy," Sam soothed. The older horse took another step toward Moon Shadow and blew through her lips while shaking her head.

Everyone looked on in silence as the mare paused, her ears moving forward and back as if she were undecided what to do. After a moment, she took the last few steps that separated her from the filly and sniffed her from forelock to tail, nipping her on the haunches while the filly nuzzled her shoulder.

Finally, Moon Shadow staggered to the mare's flank, but as she stretched her neck to drink, the mustang mare shifted her hips in the opposite direction and squealed once more.

Old Harvey placed his gnarled hands on the fence and spoke to the wild one. "Don't be like that, sis," he scolded. "This little filly needs your help."

"Give her some time," Sam said.

They watched for several more minutes while the mare continued to nuzzle the filly, but moved away every time Moon Shadow tried to nurse.

"This could be why her own foal isn't with her," Harvey said. "Some new mommas are ticklish and they won't let their foals nurse. It's possible that's how her foal died."

After several more minutes of shuffling around, Moon

Shadow boldly reached under the mare's belly. The mustang immediately squealed and kicked, sending the foal toppling into the dirt.

"No!" Callie shouted. She threw open the gate for the mare to leave. "Get her out of there before Moon Shadow gets hurt!"

Sam nodded and Justin sent the lasso flying toward the mare's hindquarters, forcing her to move toward the gate. Moon Shadow scrambled to her feet and tried to follow, but Callie slammed the gate closed before she reached it.

The filly gave a lonesome whinny. It sounded so forlorn that Callie felt as if someone had punched her right in the heart. She wanted to run to the little buckskin foal and scoop her up in her arms and tell her that everything was going to be all right.

But everything *wasn't* going to be all right. Moon Shadow's mother was dead and the other horses didn't want her. She was an outcast.

Sam made his way over to where Callie stood, his spurs jingling as his boots hit the packed dirt of the pen. He leaned on the rail and stroked his thick mustache as he stared at Callie. "Well…" he drawled. "Bottle-feeding an orphaned foal is a lot of work and a big responsibility. Are you serious about this?"

Callie nodded vigorously. At this moment, there was nothing she wanted more than to take care of Moon Shadow.

The cowboy continued to study her, and Callie fidgeted under his gaze. Did he think she was too young to take on such a task? Or that she didn't know enough about orphaned foals?

Justin coiled his rope. "Are you up to bottle-feeding around the clock?" At Callie's nod he continued, "It's a good thing you're on summer break, because you're going to be busier than a bear on a honey farm. It's going to be an all-day job until she's a couple months old and eating hay regularly."

Old Harvey spoke up. "You'd better find yourself a good milk goat. You can buy powdered foal milk at the feed store, but I don't think they do as well on that. Cow's milk is too rich. When I was on the payroll here, we had several goats on the property."

Susan started toward the long wooden building where extra supplies were kept. "I'll get the bottle." She turned to Harvey. "There's still a little bit of mare's milk left in the refrigerator in the main office. Could you please bring that to me?"

While Harvey hobbled off to the office, Callie helped Justin herd Moon Shadow into a smaller pen. There were no other orphans—or Leppy foals, as the people who worked with mustangs called them—on the property, so Moon Shadow would be kept separate.

"Here, let me help you catch her," Justin volunteered as he moved quietly toward the little mustang. "Stretch your arms out so she can't get past you, and we'll herd her into the corner."

Moon Shadow nickered in concern when she saw she was being approached by two humans in a crouched position. "Easy, baby," Callie crooned.

The filly made a sudden bolt, and Justin reached out to capture her in his arms. "Easy, easy," he spoke in a calming voice, holding on until the foal stopped struggling. He nodded to Callie. "Come on over and pet her. We need her to realize that nobody's going to hurt her. She's had a lot of action this morning and she's a little upset."

Callie ran her hands over the soft baby hair of the filly's trembling body. "You're going to be okay," she said. "All we want to do is help you."

"Let me show you a secret I learned from my grandfather," Justin said. He moved his face closer to the filly's head. "Have you ever seen a baby horse chew when an older horse that isn't its momma comes near?"

Callie nodded. She knew that when an older horse approached a young one, even if there was a fence between them, the baby would make a chewing motion like it was eating bubble gum with its mouth open. It made a funny, smacking sound and always made her laugh when she heard it.

"They're telling that bigger horse, 'I'm just a baby, don't hurt me,'" Justin explained. "And the older horse will usually just pin its ears or swish its tail to warn them off. They rarely hurt the baby."

Justin put his face next to the foal's muzzle and made the chewing sound. Moon Shadow instantly showed interest and pricked her little fox ears in his direction. She seemed to relax and even took an eager step forward.

"Now you try it," Justin said as he gently corralled the filly in his arms.

Callie put her face parallel with Moon Shadow's and began the chewing motion. The foal stretched her neck and blew softly on Callie's cheeks. "I think she likes me," Callie said, trying not to laugh as the filly's long curly whiskers tickled her chin.

Justin released his hold on the foal, and Moon Shadow stepped toward Callie, bobbing her head and sniffing her clothes. Callie raised her hand to pet the filly's neck, but Moon Shadow spun and ran several steps before turning to face them.

"You'll have to move slowly until she gets used to being around us," Justin said as he went to catch the filly again.

Moon Shadow was much easier to round up this time. They were still trying to make friends with her when Susan returned with the milk. She handed the bottle to Callie. "Since you're going to be doing the work, you might as well start right now. I know you've bottle-fed calves before. This should be a little easier, because foals don't usually butt you with their heads."

Callie gave a short laugh. She remembered being knocked over by one of the bull calves her parents were raising. Feeding Moon Shadow would definitely be easier.

But the little mustang proved them wrong. Every time Callie tried to get Moon Shadow to accept the bottle, she spit out the rubber nipple. Justin and the vet stayed around for a while trying to help, but eventually they had to go finish other jobs around the pens.

"Just keep trying," Susan encouraged. "We'll be back to check on you in a while. I'll send Harvey over to help you. He used to work with the orphaned foals."

While Callie waited for Harvey, she spoke softly to Moon Shadow, smiling when the filly curled out her tongue and made sucking noises. "You look like you're hungry enough to eat all of this, even if it is in a bottle. Why won't you drink?" She tipped the bottle up and poured some of the milk on her fingers and tasted a drop with her tongue. It wasn't the best thing she'd ever tried, but it wasn't too bad. She slowly raised her hand and rubbed the little buckskin's soft coat. "We'll make a good team, you and I," she said softly as she picked up the bottle again. "Now, if I can just get you to eat."

Moon Shadow made more sucking sounds with her tongue. Milk was still dripping from Callie's hand, so she offered it to the filly. To her surprise, Moon Shadow sucked the milk from her fingers. Callie picked up the bottle and tried again, but the foal immediately spit it out. "Okay, we'll do it your way," she said, pouring more milk over her fingers. She giggled as the foal's soft tongue tickled her hand.

"It looks like you're making progress," Harvey said as his cane tapped across the packed earth of the roadway that circled the mustang pens. He was carrying a bucket, but Callie couldn't see what was inside.

"What do you have there?" she asked.

Harvey took the unlit corncob pipe he kept clamped in his jaws and shoved it in his front pocket. He smiled, showing off his new false teeth. "I managed to round up some goat's milk. I figured it might come in handy," he said as he hung his cane on the side of the pen and let himself in through the gate.

Callie shook her head. "This isn't going well at all. Moon Shadow won't drink from the bottle. The best she'll do is suck on my fingers."

Harvey set the milk bucket down near the filly. "She doesn't have to drink out of the bottle," he said. "If you can get her to drink from a bucket, it'll be even better."

"What do we have here?" an impatient voice questioned from the far side of the fence.

Callie's head swung around at the sound of the familiar nasally voice. The boss man of the Antelope Springs Mustang Facility stood outside Moon Shadow's pen, staring in at them. Callie always felt creeped-out whenever Ron Jeffers was around.

The man's small, pig eyes made him look mean and unintelligent. And the frown on his long, pointed face made it clear: he was not very pleased.

Callie knew from the gossip she'd heard around the pens that Mr. Jeffers didn't like the hassle of attending to orphan foals. He felt his hired hands could be put to better use.

"We've got ourselves an orphan," Harvey said.

Callie's stomach sank. She wanted to kick Harvey right in the shins for making such a blunder. But the old man's mind wasn't what it used to be. He'd obviously forgotten how Mr. Jeffers felt about orphans.

Nine

❧

Mr. Jeffers leaned his thin frame on the fence. His eyes got even smaller as he scowled in Harvey's direction. "What do you mean, '*we*'?" he scoffed. "You haven't been on our payroll in years. You're a visitor here who helps out every now and then. Don't forget that your *visitor's* privileges can be revoked at any time."

Harvey blanched at the rude remark, but he turned back to Moon Shadow without responding to Mr. Jeffers.

How could anyone be such a jerk to a nice old man? Callie wondered.

"I take it that broom-tail didn't make it last night," Mr. Jeffers observed. "It's unfortunate that her filly survived."

"Don't say that!" Callie cried, feeling as if Mr. Jeffers had just slapped her across the face.

The boss man cleared his throat and smiled condescendingly. "What I meant to say was, some foals in her situation die anyway. It takes a lot of time to care for an orphan and I'm short on man-power already." He cleared his throat. "I can't afford to have someone watching this mustang around the clock. I've got over three hundred other horses here to take care of, and a new batch that just came in. It's hardly worth the man-hours we'd have to put in to save her."

Callie clenched and unclenched her fists. She was so angry she couldn't speak. It was a good thing, too, because what she wanted to say to Mr. Jeffers at this moment would probably get her banned from the mustang pens and grounded by her parents for life.

Harvey caught her eyes, warning her with a quirk of his brow to stay silent. He softly stroked Moon Shadow's coat and spoke over his shoulder to Mr. Jeffers. "This filly won't be any trouble to you, sir. The girl and I will get her eating on her own. Callie has volunteered to take care of her."

Mr. Jeffers gave them a doubtful look. "You can't really expect me to believe that this girl's parents are going to let her stay out here around the clock to care for this orphan?"

Callie had to admit that Mr. Jeffers had a point. Her parents probably wouldn't let her spend the night at the mustang pens unless one of them was with her, and she doubted she could talk her parents into sleeping on hay bales in a sleeping bag.

"We could take her back to my place," Callie said hopefully. "We've got plenty of room, and it might make things easier." Bringing Moon Shadow to their farm would be the perfect solution! Her parents were all for volunteer projects. And the best part was, it would give them time to get to know Moon Shadow and fall in love with her before she broached the subject of adopting the filly.

Mr. Jeffers shook his head. "This mustang is government property. You'd have to adopt her in order to take her home. Do you have the $125 fee to adopt this mustang?"

Harvey's head snapped around. "In the past, we've given these Leppy foals away to a good adoptive home."

Mr. Jeffers shook his head. "This isn't the past, old-timer. You know our rules. You can only adopt a mustang if you're eighteen or older and have the right kind of fencing and housing, *and* you pay the adoption fee." He nodded to Callie. "If you want to adopt this filly, I'll send the paperwork down to you, and you can bring your parents around tomorrow to write out the check. No exceptions." He turned and stalked toward the office.

Callie let out the breath she'd been holding.

"Don't pay him no never-mind." Harvey lapsed into old cowboy talk as he took the unlit corncob pipe from his front pocket and clamped it between his teeth, his eyes drilling holes in Mr. Jeffer's back. "There goes a scoundrel if I ever did see one. You'd do well to stay clear of him, young lady."

Callie couldn't resist sticking her tongue out at the retreating Mr. Jeffers. Harvey gave a hearty laugh, startling Moon Shadow, who jumped sideways and almost knocked over the milk bucket.

"Whoa, sis," the old man crooned. He gathered the filly between his arms and cradled her while Callie offered some more milk on her fingers. "That's it," Harvey instructed. "Now, each time she takes the milk, just drop your hand a little lower into the bucket."

Callie did as she was told. Within another ten minutes, Moon Shadow was sucking milk from the small pail. "She's got it!" Callie crowed in triumph.

Dr. Susan walked up and leaned her elbows on the fence. "Looks like Harvey's been teaching you some of his tricks."

Callie smiled broadly. "Isn't it great? Now that she knows how to eat, she can be adopted. Mr. Jeffers said he'd send the adoption paperwork down later."

Susan slapped her a high-five through the bars of the corral. "I don't think you'll have any problems being approved," she said, "as long as your mom and dad sign for you. Underage kids are allowed to care for a mustang under their parents' approval, but the horse can't be put into your name until you're eighteen." She took off her glasses and cleaned the lenses on her shirttail. "The trouble is going to be in trying to convince your parents that you need this filly. Your dad was just here a few minutes ago to pick up Celah. I was going to mention something to him then, to see if maybe I could soften him up, but he was in a big hurry to get home. He said something about not being able to get the right parts for the tractor."

Callie felt the hope drain out of her like water out of a leaky trough. A broken tractor meant more money going out the door. Who was she kidding? Her parents would never let her adopt Moon Shadow. It would be years before the tiny mustang could pull her own weight. Callie took a deep breath. She would not cry in front of Harvey and Susan. Things would work out. They just *had* to!

"Would you like me to come in and talk to your parents when I drop you off tonight?" Susan volunteered.

Callie wanted to leap at the offer, but she knew her mom and dad. If she wanted this badly enough, she'd have to go to them by herself and plead her case. She only had a couple more hours to come up with the right thing to say. How could she convince her parents that Moon Shadow would be a worthy addition to their family?

She really needed to call Billie when she got home. Her friend was good at saying just the right thing. Callie felt a momentary pang of guilt. Billie was her best friend, but she'd been so worried about Moon Shadow that she hadn't even bothered to call her. That would have to be the first thing on her list when she arrived home. Hopefully, Billie could help her find a way to convince her parents to let her adopt Moon Shadow.

Callie removed the empty milk bucket, smiling at the way the little buckskin followed her back to the fence. "Thanks a lot, Harvey," she said as she handed the pail through the fence to Susan.

Susan opened the gate for her. "We've got some more bumps and bruises to doctor on the new horses. You've got another two hours before you have to feed again. Let's see if we can get this done and knock off early today."

Callie waved good-bye to Harvey and followed Susan back to the sick pen. Justin was waiting for them with a handful of papers.

"So, you're really going to do it?" Justin asked as he turned over the adoption forms to Callie.

She shrugged. "I'm going to try, but I don't think my parents are going to say yes."

"How about if my dad and I take care of Moon Shadow again tonight?" Justin asked. "That way you can stay home and work on your parents." He gave her a thumbs-up sign. "I'll be rooting for you."

"That'd be great," Callie said. "Thanks." She watched as the young cowboy walked away. She wished that she could be the one to stay and feed Moon Shadow, but she knew she'd have to get her parents' permission first.

Callie shoved the papers into her pocket and went to help Susan. They finished the sick pen in just under two hours, so Callie had a chance to hurry back to Moon Shadow while Susan got ready to leave. Harvey had another bucket of milk waiting for her when she reached the filly's pen.

"This one has some powdered milk substitute mixed in with the goat's milk," he said. "We need to stretch the milk we've got, and we're not sure if you'll be able to get a goat right away. We'd best get her used to the powdered stuff now."

Callie walked into the pen, and Moon Shadow shuffled over in her unsteady gait. "Shouldn't she be getting stronger by now?" Callie asked in concern.

Harvey handed her the bucket. "This little girl has been through quite an ordeal. She was born before her time, and all of the stress her mother went through during that roundup didn't help her any. Her health will probably be touch-and-go for a while. We'll have to watch her closely. Sometimes these orphans seem like they're doing fine, and then all of a sudden they go downhill."

Callie offered the milk to Moon Shadow. The filly fumbled around the edge of the bucket, her velvety-soft nose bumping Callie's hand as she lipped the sides of the pail.

"You're supposed to put your head *into* the bucket," Callie said as she tried to guide Moon Shadow to the milk. But the filly continued to work her mouth around the lip of the pail. Finally, Callie resorted to dipping her fingers in the milk again and offering the feast to Moon Shadow. It took a couple of tries, but eventually, the filly was drinking on her own again.

Moon Shadow

Susan pulled her truck to a stop outside of the pen and rolled down her window. "Is everything all right?"

Callie nodded. "Justin and his father are going to take care of Moon Shadow tonight while I go home and figure a way to convince my parents to let me adopt her. I'll be ready to go as soon as Moon Shadow finishes her lunch."

Callie stared into the filly's soft brown eyes, smiling at the slurping noises the orphan made while drinking her milk. She wished this moment could go on forever. The truth was, she didn't want to go home and face the adoption battle with her parents. She was afraid it was a war she couldn't win.

Ten

꧁✲꧂

Callie borrowed Susan's cell phone to call Billie on the way home. She could tell that her friend was a little hurt that she hadn't called sooner, but after she heard about all that had happened, Billie understood. She was excited that Callie might have a chance to adopt the newborn foal. "Don't try to finagle your parents into anything," she said. "They won't buy it. Just tell them the truth and hope they realize how much Moon Shadow means to you." Callie knew it was good advice.

Susan pulled into the driveway and Callie climbed out of the truck. "Thanks for the lift," she said.

"Are you sure you don't want me to come in with you and help you talk to your parents?" the veterinarian offered.

Callie shook her head and waved good-bye to Susan. She wasn't ready to ask her parents about Moon Shadow just yet. She needed to have all of the details straight before she approached them. This was too important to risk their saying no before she even had a chance to explain.

She looked around the property. Celah wasn't in the front paddock. The tractor sat near the barn with several of its parts strewn on the ground. It looked as if her father hadn't been able to fix the old John Deere.

Because of the late snows this year, her parents were already behind schedule with the planting. Now they would have to use horsepower to get the job done, and Celah couldn't work as fast as the old tractor.

"Callie, we're back here!" her father hollered from the plot of land he was working.

"Poor Celah," Callie muttered. It was warm and she could see the lather under the mare's collar from where she stood. When her parents were finished plowing, she'd give the mare a bath and take her out to graze on the small patch of grass that was supposed to be their front lawn. It would give her more time to decide how to approach them about adopting Moon Shadow.

"Do you need help?" Callie volunteered.

Her mother looked up from the batch of plants they'd been growing in the greenhouse all spring and waved her off. "Go make yourself a sandwich, honey. Then you can come out and help me put the rest of these in the ground."

Callie nodded and trotted off to the kitchen. She'd make herself a quick peanut-butter-and-honey sandwich and look over the adoption information booklet Mr. Jeffers had given her.

She kicked off her boots at the back door and entered the house, placing the paperwork on the counter. After washing her hands, she took out a loaf of whole-wheat bread that her mother had made the night before and made a sandwich, then rummaged through the refrigerator for something to drink. "Yuck!" She wrinkled her nose at the fresh carrot juice her father had made with the juicer. Pushing aside the vegetables on the bottom shelf, she reached for a root beer she had hidden there. "That's more like it." She grinned as she gathered her things and headed for her room.

Balancing the sandwich, soda, and adoption papers, Callie made her way down the hall and pushed her bedroom door open with her shoulder. She set everything on her dresser and spread the adoption information across the hand-stitched quilt. Sitting cross-legged in the middle of her bed, she took a bite of her sandwich and opened the brochure, quickly scanning the requirements for adopting Moon Shadow.

Immediately she began to frown. They'd need a stock-type trailer to haul the filly. Her family didn't own *any* type of horse trailer. They'd have to borrow one from a neighbor. Strike one in the ball game she was about to play with her parents.

The Bureau of Land Management also required a five-foot fence for foals, and a six-foot fence for grown horses. That was one thing in her favor. With Celah measuring eighteen hands, all of their corral fencing was extra tall.

She read the next paragraph and frowned again. They'd need a twelve-by-twelve stall to house the filly. All of the smaller stalls in their barn had been taken out years ago to make room for the tractor and several tons of hay. Celah had her own twenty-foot stall, which they'd made by taking out the partition of two of the smaller stalls. It would be necessary to build Moon Shadow her own place in another corner of the barn. Strike two.

And last but not least, the $125 adoption fee.

Strike three.

The peanut butter balled in Callie's throat, making it almost impossible to swallow. She felt the sting of tears against the back of her eyes. The odds seemed insurmountable. They didn't have the extra money to adopt Moon Shadow and build a new stall, let alone pay for the medical attention the filly would need, the milk goat, and the powdered milk mix they'd need to feed her for the next few months until she could be transferred to a diet of all hay.

But Callie knew she had to try. Her parents were expecting her to help with the planting. Now would probably be the best time to ask. She gathered the rest of her uneaten sandwich and empty root beer can and tossed them in the garbage before going outside to put on her boots.

She walked slowly toward the east garden, her mind churning with what she was going to say.

"So how's the little mustang? Mrs. McLean asked as she looked up from one of the evenly plowed rows.

Callie tried to be courageous and say exactly what was on her mind, but she didn't have the nerve to ask the big question just yet. Instead she took the wheelbarrow from her mother and rolled it toward the greenhouse to get the next load of zucchini. "She's doing okay. Susan says she's got a good chance of making it if she gets constant care," she said over her shoulder as she hightailed it toward the glass building. Then she parked the wheelbarrow inside the big door and kicked herself for being such a coward.

She reached for the small pots of zucchini seedlings and loaded them into the wheelbarrow. Tonight over dinner would be the best time to ask about Moon Shadow. Right now she needed to put in a good day's work to prove to her parents how responsible she could be.

It was late afternoon and the sun beat down on the back of Callie's neck as she sank her hands into the rich dirt and packed the new plants into place. She was about to reach for a gallon-sized tomato when Celah stopped plowing the tract and whinnied so loudly that her sides shook. The call was answered by a high-pitched neigh, and Callie looked up to see a small red pony trotting down the road. The riderless Shetland turned up their driveway and broke into a canter at the sight of another horse.

"Whoa!" Her father steadied the lines as Celah sidestepped a couple of rows and turned her head, trying to see around the blinkers on her bridle.

The pony trotted across their newly planted rows, taking out several yellow squash and a tomato before Callie put her arms around his neck and stopped him from doing more damage.

"I'll get a rope," her mother said, taking off for the barn at a jog. She quickly returned and fashioned a makeshift halter for the little gelding.

Callie recognized Jake, the pony Luke Thompson and his older sister Jill used to ride when they were little. The Shetland had been retired when the Thompson kids graduated to the fancy quarter horses their father raised, and Jake had spent the rest of his retirement learning how to become an escape artist.

"It looks like you did it again," Callie said as she ruffled the Shetland's fuzzy mane. "I'll walk him back to the Thompsons' when we're done," she told her parents.

Her father moved Celah back to the row he had been plowing. "I've only got a bit left to finish," he said. "If you wait, we can tie Jake to the back of the pickup to trot him home."

Callie looked at the gray hairs growing on the pony's face and flanks. "The mile to the Thompsons' is a pretty long distance for this old guy to trot behind the truck. It's too bad we can't pick him up and put him in the back." She gave Jake another pat and turned back to her mom. "I'll tie him in the barn and give him some hay while we finish up. Then I'll walk him down."

Mrs. McLean shaded her eyes and glanced at the late afternoon sun. "Maybe you'd better get going now," she suggested, reaching out to wipe a smudge of dirt off of Callie's face. "Your father and I can plant the rest of these tomatoes. We'll come get you in the truck when we're done."

Callie gave a tug on Jake's halter as he stretched his lips to grab another tomato plant. "Let's go, you old Houdini horse."

A slight breeze blew across the late afternoon landscape as Callie and Jake hit the road. The sharp smell of bitterbrush filled the air, and she inhaled deeply, enjoying the sights and sounds of the desert preparing for nightfall. Several scrub jays flitted back and forth on the sagebrush, chattering happily, and the low hum of deerflies made Jake swish his tail in agitation.

As they walked, Callie talked to the pony, practicing what she hoped to say to her parents later on. She had to adopt Moon Shadow. She feared for the filly's well-being if she didn't. Mr. Jeffers obviously didn't want to take the time that Moon Shadow needed, and it would be tough to find anyone else willing to adopt an orphan foal that would require around-the-clock care for weeks. If she didn't adopt the little mustang, there was a chance that Moon Shadow might become sickly and die.

Callie felt her heart squeeze. She'd already lost Moonbeam. The thought of losing her foal was too much. Somehow she'd find a way to convince her parents. She prayed that she'd come up with the right words and the courage to use them.

They rounded the bend in the dirt road, and the Thompson ranch came into view. Callie was always awestruck when she visited this place. The ranch house was a huge, two-story affair with tall rock chimneys at each end and a wraparound porch. Quaking aspen had been planted when the ranch was built several decades ago. The graceful trees now towered over the house, providing shade during the long hot summer and making soothing, whispering noises when the wind blew.

The ranch house was nice, but Callie's favorite building was the barn. It was spectacular. Built a year ago—after the hundred-mile-per-hour zephyr winds tore off the roof and a wall of the old barn—it sported twenty-four stalls, a tack room, a feed room, a wash rack with hot and cold water, and a saddling area. Mr. Thompson and his wife had given Callie a personal tour last winter when she had returned Jake from another one of his escapades.

The outside of the barn was white like the house, but the inside was a beautiful golden pine, varnished to a shine. On each stall was a plaque engraved with a horse's name, and on a peg outside each stall hung a beautiful leather halter.

Luke's sister Jill was riding in the outdoor arena when Callie walked by with the pony in tow. Jill was an amazing rider. She was two grades ahead of Callie and Luke and attended the high school next door to their school. Callie admired Jill, but suspected that the teenager didn't even know she was alive. Someday, she hoped to be as good a rider as Jill.

Jake gave a shrill whinny of hello to Jill's chestnut mare. The tall pretty girl with the long blonde hair halted her horse and turned to look at Callie and the pony. She gave Callie a knowing smile. "Looks like our little trouble-maker went visiting again," she said. "My dad's in the barn." She turned her horse in a perfect half-circle on the hind and trotted off.

Callie almost felt as if she'd been dismissed. Jill's tone was kind, though, Callie reminded herself; she'd even smiled at her. *Maybe the next time I see her,* Callie thought, *I'll be brave enough to say hello.*

"Well, well, what do we have here?" Mr. Thompson said, strolling from the barn with his cell phone held to his ear. He put up his hand to signal Callie that he'd be right with her.

Callie scratched Jake's ears while she waited for the short, stocky man to finish his conversation.

Mr. Thompson closed the phone. "Good to see you again, Callie. I see Jake's been up to his old tricks," he said as he took the makeshift halter and lead. "I'm sorry you had to walk all the way down here. We're short a couple of stable hands. Luke's been helping, but he's not the best at locking gates and stall doors...or cleaning stalls and raking the shed row, either," he said with a chuckle.

It didn't surprise Callie that Luke was such lousy help. He was really lazy with his schoolwork, too. She followed Mr. Thompson into the barn and helped him put the pony back in his large box stall.

Mr. Thompson turned the pony loose and returned the rope to Callie. "I don't suppose you'd know anyone who'd be interested in cleaning stalls for me?"

He made the offer in a joking manner, but it immediately gave Callie an idea. "I could do it, Mr. Thompson," she blurted out.

The horse breeder raised an eyebrow. "Callie, you're barely big enough to push that wheelbarrow when it's empty," he teased.

"No, really, I can do it," she insisted. Before she knew it, her mouth was running faster then Cloud Dancer's herd across the open desert. She told Mr. Thompson everything, starting with Moonbeam dying and ending with her plan to rescue Moon Shadow. "But to do it," she said, "I'm going to need to earn some money."

Mr. Thompson paused, rubbing the stubble on his cheek. "That's quite a story you've got there, little lady." He ran a hand through his short-cropped, graying hair and took another long moment to decide what he wanted to do. "I'll tell you what. I'll give you a two-week trial to see if you can handle the job. And just because you brought ol' Jake home, I'll front you the adoption money for your mustang foal."

"What mustang foal?" Luke's head poked around the corner of the barn. "She doesn't have a mustang foal." He looked at Callie. "And why would anybody want an old broom-tail anyway?" He picked up a rock and chucked it toward the manure pile with a smart-aleck grin. "Oh, yeah—some people can't *afford* a decent horse."

"All right, son, that's enough!" Mr. Thompson snapped.

Callie glared at Luke and her fists balled at her sides. She wanted to push him straight into the manure pile. So what if she couldn't afford one of the Thompsons' stupid quarter horses? Moon Shadow was just as beautiful as any of those pampered purebred horses.

"Dad..." Luke began.

"Not another word," Mr. Thompson said sharply. "Get back to

your stalls." He turned to Callie. "I apologize for my boy. Sometimes he opens his mouth before he thinks."

That's the understatement of the year, Callie thought.

"Don't pay any attention to Luke," Mr. Thompson continued. "Just because a horse doesn't have a pedigree doesn't mean that it can't have value or talent." He pointed to an old horse in the far corral. "See that bay over there? He's one of the best roping horses I've ever had. You might think that he comes from our breeding stock, but that old boy came out of the Virginia Range."

Callie's head snapped up. "That horse is a mustang?"

Mr. Thompson nodded. "When he turns, you can see the freeze brand on his neck. The mustangs have had a long, rich history here in America, starting with the first load of Spanish barbs the Spaniards brought over in the 1500s. Rather than haul those horses back across the sea when they returned home, they turned them loose to fend for themselves."

Callie smiled. She'd heard this story several times from old Harvey, but she never grew tired of it.

"The mustangs survived on their own for hundreds of years, and they were doing just fine." Mr. Thompson seemed to enjoy having an appreciative audience. Callie was sure that Luke didn't have the patience to listen to his dad for more than a few seconds. "Until man had to step in and start messing things up, of course. During the Civil War, the military turned draft stallions out with the mustang herds, hoping to build up their size so they'd be of better use to the military. And up until 1971, when the federal government stepped in with a law to protect the mustang, ranchers would go out and shoot the mustang stallions and put blooded horses in their place. They were trying to make a better ranch horse for working cattle."

He pointed to the old bay in the far corral. "Ol' Butch out there probably shares some of the same blood as my registered horses. If you get a good mustang and work really hard to earn its trust, it'll make a great horse."

"That's what I'm hoping," Callie said, nodding eagerly. Moon Shadow would be a wonderful horse if she got the chance to raise her. And now that Mr. Thompson had given her a job, she had a lot better chance of getting her parents to say yes.

"Come on," Mr. Thompson said as he fished the keys to his big blue truck out of his pocket. "I'll give you a ride home. I don't want you to be too tired to start work tomorrow."

Callie climbed into the shiny new vehicle and sighed in relief. Things were definitely looking up. Now all she had to do was convince her parents that Moon Shadow would be a great addition to their family.

Eleven

hanks for the ride, Mr. Thompson." Callie waved good-
bye and walked up the driveway to her house. She could
see her father out by the barn giving Celah a bath. Her
mother was just putting away the wheelbarrow. Callie smiled as
she kicked off her boots by the back door. She finally had some
bargaining chips now.

As she opened the door the smell of pot roast drifted in from
the kitchen, making her mouth water. She quickly changed her
clothes and set the table for dinner. Her parents soon joined
her.

"That was nice of Mr. Thompson to bring you home," Mrs.
McLean said. "We were just getting ready to come get you." She
washed her hands in the sink, then took down a large serving
bowl from the cupboard.

Callie poured the milk and took her chair at their small, cloth-
covered table, waiting for her mom to dish up the food. She
swung her feet back and forth, bumping them on the chair leg as
she waited for the right time to broach the subject of adopting the
orphaned mustang. Her mother set a plate of meat, potatoes, and

carrots in front of her, but Callie couldn't bring herself to take a bite. Instead, she pushed the carrots around on the plate and cut the pot roast into a hundred small pieces.

Her mother gave her a sideways glance, but Callie held her tongue. The moment wasn't right yet.

"So how did things go at the mustang pens this morning?" her father asked as he helped himself to another portion of meat and potatoes. "I heard you tell your mother that the little filly is still alive."

Callie nodded. "Moon Shadow's drinking milk now," she said proudly. "Harvey and I taught her how to lap up goat's milk from a bucket, so at least she's eating on her own." She nudged her full plate away. "But Mr. Jeffers doesn't want to have to take care of an orphan. He says he doesn't have the manpower to do it. I'm afraid of what's going to happen to her." She waited to see what her parents would say.

Mrs. McLean pushed Callie's plate back toward her and motioned for her to eat. "I'm sure with all of the wild horse organizations around here, they won't have any trouble finding a good home for Moon Shadow."

Callie dropped her fork on her plate with a clang. "N...no!" she sputtered. "That's not what I meant!"

Both of her parents stared at her in confusion. "Why wouldn't you want someone to adopt her, Callie?" her mother said. "I'm sure she's going to need constant care for quite a while. If Mr. Jeffers doesn't want to do it, it would be better to give the filly to someone else."

Callie took a deep breath. "*I* want to be the one to take care of Moon Shadow."

"But you *are* taking care of her, dear." Mrs. McLean smiled and folded her napkin, clearly not understanding what Callie was getting at.

"Mom...Dad... I want to *adopt* Moon Shadow." Callie turned to her father, hoping to find an ally, but he looked just as surprised as her mother.

"We can't afford another horse," Mr. McLean said flatly. "Especially a horse that could have a lot of medical problems. It's hard enough just feeding Celah."

"But Moon Shadow wouldn't eat much," Callie protested, looking from one parent to the other. Neither of them looked agreeable to the idea.

"I can pay for everything," Callie continued quickly. "I have a job now. Mr. Thompson hired me to clean stalls." She pushed her plate away once more. Her appetite was totally gone. "He said he'd pay for Moon Shadow's adoption fee and he'd take it out of my paycheck. It won't cost you guys anything." She turned to her mom, then her dad. "Please say yes," she begged. "I can do this. I know I can! Moon Shadow's going to be a great horse." She chewed her bottom lip as she waited for their response.

Mr. McLean folded his napkin and laid it on the table. "Callie..."

"Please, Dad!" This wasn't the way she had hoped the conversation would go. "Moon Shadow is so little and helpless. She needs me!"

"But Callie," her mother interrupted, "that filly will probably always be little and weak. If you're really serious about getting a horse, maybe you could save up your money from cleaning stalls and buy an animal that has potential. You know, something you could take to the local 4-H shows, and use to help us with the farm."

"And remember the old saying," her father added. "It costs as much to feed a good horse as it does a bad one."

Callie sat there stunned, feeling as if she had just been bucked off and stomped on. *Moon Shadow, a bad horse?* How could her parents say such a thing? "Why do people say things like that about mustangs?" she said hotly. "Just because they don't have a pedigree doesn't mean they can't be good horses! You've seen some of the beautiful mustangs that roam the hills around here."

She pushed away from the table and stood up so quickly that her chair toppled over backwards. Her heart was pounding against her rib cage and there was a roar like a waterfall inside her head. She knew she should bend down and pick up the chair, but at that moment all she could see was her dream of owning Moon Shadow slipping away.

"It's not fair!" she cried, her voice rising to a level of hysteria. "I want this so badly and I've got the money to do it. You're just being mean!"

By the stricken look on her mother's face, Callie knew she'd gone too far, but it was too late to stop. She felt the horrible words tumbling out of her mouth and she couldn't stop them. "The kids around here see our little-bitty house and all the junk in our yard and they make fun of me. They laugh at my clothes and think I'm just some dorky hippie kid who's not good enough to be friends with. Just because we don't have as much money as they do, they think they're better than me. But I get better grades than all of them!"

Tears sprang to her eyes and she wiped at them angrily. "I'm kind of like Moon Shadow. I don't have a fancy pedigree worth a lot of money, so the other kids think I'm not good enough." She plucked at her new shirt in agitation. One of the buttons popped off and rolled across the floor.

As the sound of the plastic button skittering across the hardwood floor faded to total silence, Callie saw the hurt expression on her parents' faces. She'd really blown it this time. She looked down at her shirt, which now had a torn sleeve. Not only had she wrecked her clothing, but she'd also done a darned good job of tearing up her mom and dad's feelings.

Callie kept her eyes down, afraid to look at her parents. She could feel the sob creeping up in her throat. Without warning, she burst into tears and ran to her room, where she threw herself on the bed and buried her face in the pillow. It was bad enough that she'd never realize her dream of owning Moon Shadow, but now she'd been horrible and disrespectful to her parents. Recalling the sadness on their faces made her cry even harder.

She wasn't sure how long she stayed there on the bed, but her tears were almost gone. The only things left were the hiccups, puffed-up eyes, and stuffy nose. Callie felt a sudden weight on the edge of her bed and opened her swollen eyes to see her mother perched there. She had thought she was done crying, but more tears rose and rushed down her cheeks.

"Don't cry, honey," her mother said softly, reaching out to stroke Callie's hair.

"I…I'm so sorry, Mom," Callie stammered between sobs. "I said some really rotten things. I didn't mean it about my clothes.

I know how hard you work to make them, and I do like them...well, most of them. Just not the tie-dyed stuff," she added with a loud sniff.

"Shhh," Mrs. McLean said, handing her daughter a tissue to dry her eyes. "I know how difficult it is to be a kid sometimes, especially when you don't have all the luxuries that some of the other kids have, but you've been a pretty good daughter so far. Why don't we just let this one slip, okay?" She wiped a tear from Callie's cheek. "Maybe we'll even take a trip into town next week and see if there's anything at that new superstore you might like."

Callie sat up and blew her nose. "Is Dad really mad?" she said in a small voice. "I said some pretty ugly things about the house and yard."

Her mother handed her another tissue. "Well, I suppose we're both a little hurt, but we'll get over it." She brushed Callie's hair off her tear-soaked face. "Here's what we've decided to do."

Callie sighed. This was it. She was going to be grounded for life.

"Your father and I have decided to let you adopt that little mustang," Mrs. McLean said.

Callie's head snapped up in surprise.

Her mother smiled. "He's always so worried about you falling off Celah in the desert somewhere and getting hurt. I convinced him that Moon Shadow won't grow to be very tall." She gave Callie a wink. "Besides, you were right. We weren't giving that filly, or you, a chance to prove yourselves. There's no reason why Moon Shadow couldn't turn out to be the best horse in the world. And you do have a job now to pay for her. Plus," she went on with a grin, "a man stopped by today and made your father an offer on that old junk car we've got parked in the side yard. That'll give us a little extra cushion to fall back on."

Callie couldn't believe her ears. They were going to let her adopt Moon Shadow! She started to cry all over again.

Mrs. McLean lifted Callie's chin. "Why all the tears, Cal? I thought that would make you really happy."

Callie threw her arms around her mother's neck. "I *am* really happy, but I was so mean to you and Dad. I don't deserve this."

Her mother hugged her back. "Well, you do owe your father an apology, and you just earned yourself another five wheelbarrow loads of weed pulling."

Callie started to laugh and a hiccup came out instead. "I'll punish myself even more and make it ten loads." She finished her hug and sat up straight. "I really am sorry I said such stupid things," she said. "I promise I'll make it up to you and Dad. You'll be proud of Moon Shadow and me."

"Well, go wash your face and get back down to supper," Mrs. McLean said, standing up. "You've still got a whole plate of food to finish and a father to thank for being so understanding."

Callie jumped off the bed. She really did have the best parents in the world. Now it was up to her to make sure they weren't sorry that they'd agreed to let her adopt Moon Shadow.

Twelve

❦

The next day, when Callie finished working for Mr. Thompson, he gave her a ride to the mustang pens. She'd called Harvey earlier to tell him the good news, and to make sure that Justin could take care of Moon Shadow until she could get there with the adoption papers.

"Well, here we are," Mr. Thompson said as he let Callie out at the main office. "You did a great job today, kiddo. I think maybe you're a good influence on Luke. He seems to work harder when you're around."

Callie grinned. "That's because he doesn't want a girl to beat him at anything."

Mr. Thompson let out a hearty laugh. "Well, whatever it takes to get that boy working is fine with me." He took out his checkbook and quickly scribbled across the paper, then handed it to Callie. "Here's your check for the mustang, young lady. You did such a good job today that I think I'll do away with that trial period and just say you're hired right now."

"Wow, thanks, Mr. Thompson!" Callie said as she jumped down from his truck. "Your giving me a job is the main reason my parents agreed to let me adopt Moon Shadow. I promise to work really hard."

"I'm sure you will," the ranch owner said as he waved good-bye and turned his truck around.

Callie hurried up the long dirt road that led to Moon Shadow's pen. Justin and his father were working the stallion corral when she arrived. Sam signaled for his son to finish what he was doing, then they both rode over to the gate.

The older cowboy tipped his hat and looked down at her from atop his big gelding. "You come to claim that buckskin filly?" he asked in a teasing tone.

Callie couldn't help but grin. "You bet. My mom and dad filled out the paperwork this morning, and Mr. Thompson wrote me the check and said he'd haul her for me. All I have to do now is turn everything in to Mr. Jeffers."

"That's awesome!" Justin said. He leaned down from his horse to slap Callie a high-five.

As Callie talked to the cowboys about how Moon Shadow had fared during the night, a car turned onto the road that led up to the mustang pens. They all watched it approach. It stopped about thirty feet from them, and a tall, willowy, blonde woman stepped out of the new Buick.

"Well, what have we here?" Sam muttered as Mr. Jeffers got out of the passenger side of the car. The boss went around and took the woman's elbow, escorting her to Moon Shadow's pen.

Callie noticed Sam's dubious look at the woman's spike heels. When Justin rolled his eyes, she wanted to laugh aloud, but she kept silent, not wanting to be rude. She was curious, though, why this city woman was visiting the mustang pens.

High heels and a dress weren't exactly common clothing at this facility.

"Everyone," Mr. Jeffers announced as he presented the woman with a flourish of his hand, "this is Theresa Midland. She's here to adopt the orphaned filly."

Callie felt her world spin and she stumbled back against the corral fence. She must have misunderstood. But the shocked and angry look on her friends' faces told her that she had heard Mr. Jeffers correctly. He had sold her down the river. Moon Shadow was going to be adopted by someone else!

Callie felt the brutal sting of betrayal. She gasped as she tried to catch her breath.

Mr. Jeffers put his hand through the fence, beckoning the little buckskin closer. "Theresa…I mean, Ms. Midland, is heading up a group of people that want to rescue a mustang." He frowned when the filly gave him a suspicious swish of her tail and walked to the back of the pen. "Sam, get your kid in there and catch this animal!" He smiled apologetically to the woman.

Justin stayed on his paint gelding, looking from Mr. Jeffers to his father to Callie. It was clear he didn't want to follow this order.

"Didn't you hear me, boy?" the boss man said. "Get in there and catch that horse. I believe that's what I pay you for."

Justin stepped off his horse and wrapped the reins around a post. "But this is Callie's filly," he said.

Ms. Midland shifted uncomfortably in her high heels. "Someone else has spoken for this foal?"

"No, no," Mr. Jeffers assured her quickly. "It's first come, first served here, and it's your check that's sitting on my desk."

Callie thought she was going to be sick. How could Mr. Jeffers do this to her? He knew she wanted Moon Shadow.

Sam stepped down from his horse and cleared his throat. "No disrespect, Mr. Jeffers, but Callie put in the first claim on this orphan."

Mr. Jeffers looked down his long nose. "The kid may have *said* that she wanted to adopt this mustang, but I have no paperwork, and no check from her."

Callie finally sprang to life. "I have them right here." She stepped forward and waved her documents.

"Oh, dear," Ms. Midland said. "It seems as if there's been a mix-up."

"There's no mix-up," Mr. Jeffers said, patting the woman on the shoulder. "The girl should have gotten here an hour earlier. You beat her to it."

Sam tried again. "I thought our rules said that if two people wanted the same horse, there was to be a bidding war."

Callie cringed. The check she carried was written for $125. That was all she had—and it had been borrowed from Mr. Thompson. If she had to bid against this woman, she would surely lose.

Mr. Jeffers narrowed his eyes at the cowboy. "That may be true, but Callie wasn't anywhere around when Ms. Midland gave me her check. I've already accepted the check, and that's final. The filly belongs to the lady and her colleagues. They want to do a good deed and save a wild horse, and this little mustang needs saving. That's that." He turned away from Moon Shadow. "I'm going up to the office to get your receipt, Theresa. I'll be back shortly."

They all watched as Mr. Jeffers strolled toward the office. From the spring in his step, Callie thought he looked mighty pleased with himself.

Mr. Rosser turned to Ms. Midland. "Have you ever cared for a young horse before?"

The blonde woman smiled and shook her head. "No. This will be our first, but we've all been reading everything we can get our hands on about horses. We've got a stall set up at a boarding stable on the other side of town. That's where Charity will be living from now on."

Callie's stomach clenched. They were going to name Moon Shadow *Charity*? This time she *knew* she was going to be sick. She sank down on a nearby bale of hay and tried to take deep breaths. Neither this city woman nor her friends knew anything about horses. How could Mr. Jeffers think that Miss Midland would give Moon Shadow a better home than she could?

"Are you sure you want this *exact* filly?" Mr. Rosser said. "She's going to be an awful lot of work. She needs to be fed around the clock."

Ms. Midland laughed. "That's the point of it all," she said. "We're trying to *save* a horse. I don't want an animal that's perfect. Our goal is to save a life."

The more the woman talked, the worse Callie felt. She knew she should speak up and say something—*anything* that would change the woman's mind—but all she could do was sit there like a bump on a log feeling sorry for herself and Moon Shadow.

"Well, if it's a real hardship case you're looking for, we've got one worse off than this one," Sam said as he winked at Callie.

Ms. Midland perked up. "Worse?"

Sam nodded. "We've got a mare and her foal on the other side of the big corral that got separated from their herd when they were out on the desert. They were half-starved when we found them. The coyotes were closing in and were going to make a meal out of them when we happened along."

The woman gasped, and Callie smiled to see that she was so wrapped up in the story.

"Yes ma'am," Sam said. "Most people don't want a skinny horse. The mare is a pretty little red-and-white pinto, and her filly is almost an exact match. They desperately need someone to take them home and give them some love and groceries. If you adopt the mare, the foal goes along with her. You get two rescues for the price of one."

Everyone stood motionless while the blonde woman contemplated the situation. "Can I see them?"

Sam looked toward the office building. Mr. Jeffers was still inside. "Sure. Why don't you get in your car and drive to the other side of that big arena, and my son Justin here will show you the pair."

Callie finally found some strength and edged closer to the fence, straining to hear what Sam was telling Justin.

"Go cut that mare and foal out of that herd and put them off somewhere by themselves so this nice lady can get a good look at them," Sam said.

He waited until Ms. Midland drove off in her car, then leaned on the fence and grinned at Callie. "I've always been one for telling the truth," he said. "But every now and then, there's a good reason for stretching things just a bit. That mare *is* awfully skinny, and I'm sure there were coyotes somewhere on the

desert that would have loved to have made a meal out of them."
He took off his hat and ran a hand through his hair. "Let's hope
the lady is back here by the time the boss man returns."

Callie entered the pen with Moon Shadow. The filly nickered
and stepped forward, bobbing her head in hello. "That's my
girl," Callie said as she took the foal's head in both hands and
rubbed her fuzzy cheekbones. Moon Shadow seemed to be a bit
stronger today. But would she continue making progress if Ms.
Midland and her co-workers took over? She heaved a sigh and
turned to Sam. "Do you think your plan will work?"

He handed Callie a bucket of goat milk for Moon Shadow,
and his wind-roughened face split into a big toothy smile. "You
know, when Justin was a little tyke, he made a lot of money on a
lemonade stand he set up in the front yard. He even convinced
the most ornery man in the neighborhood that he needed a tall
glass of his lemonade. If anyone can talk that woman into that
other mare and foal, it's my son. Besides, we've done a little work
with that pair. I think those city folks will be a lot safer and better
off with that pinto mare and foal then they will with your filly."

Callie liked the sound of that. *Your filly.* She picked up the
bucket, and Moon Shadow practically walked over the top of her
to get to the milk. "It looks like you'll be needing some manners," she scolded.

Moon Shadow thrust her muzzle deep into the bucket and
drank greedily. Callie held the bucket as she kept one eye on the
office and the other on the road. She hoped the lady made it
back before Mr. Jeffers returned and figured out what they were
up to. She felt a twinge of panic when the office door opened
and the boss man stepped into the sunshine.

"Come on," Sam muttered, casting his gaze to the other side of the pens, but there was still no sign of the Buick. Mr. Jeffers walked briskly toward them, carrying some papers in his hand.

"He's going to be really angry," Callie said. "For some reason, he really wanted Ms. Midland to have Moon Shadow."

Sam stood on the fence to get a better view. "She's still looking at the mare and foal."

Callie held her breath. In another second, Mr. Jeffers would look up and see that the blue car wasn't there. He'd know they'd been up to something. Would he be so mad that he'd forbid her to return to the mustang pens? Would Justin and his dad lose their jobs? If so, it would be all her fault.

A horn sounded and a large delivery truck bumped down the dirt road toward the office. Callie began to breathe again as the truck rolled to a stop. Mr. Jeffers would have to sign for the delivery and show the driver where to put the load. That might buy them the extra time they needed.

Moon Shadow finished her milk, and Callie spent the few minutes running her hands over the filly's body, getting her accustomed to being handled.

"Here they come," Sam said.

Callie crossed her fingers, hoping that the news was good. Justin raced across the arena, bringing his horse to a sliding stop in a cloud of dust. When the dust cleared, she could tell by the look on his face that he'd been successful. She almost felt like hugging him.

A moment later, Ms. Midland stepped from her car and came to the fence, stretching her arm through the metal panels to grasp Callie's hand. "You sweet child," she said. "This young man told me the story of how you worked so hard to save this filly's life. I had no idea you wanted her, or I would have never put in the adoption papers." She pointed toward the pinto mare and foal. "Since this little buckskin is in good hands, I'll turn my attention to that pair over there. They need a lot of help, and there are more of us to take care of the two of them."

Callie smiled at her, grateful that she'd stepped aside. "Thank you, ma'am," she said. "You can always call us if you have any questions." A movement on the road caught her eye and she turned to see Mr. Jeffers walking toward them. "Uh oh. What do we do now? He's not going to be happy about this."

Ms. Midland hailed the boss with a wave of her manicured hand. She glanced back at Callie. "You let me handle Mr. Jeffers. I'll get the adoption transferred to my pintos, and then this little orphan will be ready for you to take home."

Callie watched as Ms. Midland chatted with Mr. Jeffers. He glanced at them and scowled, but a few minutes later he motioned for Callie to follow him and the lady to the office.

"We might as well get all the paperwork done at once," he said.

Callie gave Justin her best smile. It looked like Moon Shadow was finally going to be hers!

Thirteen

❦

The next day, Billie and Justin came by to help Callie and her father build the box stall for Moon Shadow. When it was finished, Callie marveled at what they had done. It was the first real thing she'd ever built and she felt very proud of her accomplishment.

Billie placed her hammer back in the toolbox and dusted off her hands. "Now all we need is Moon Shadow."

Justin checked his watch. "She should be arriving any minute now."

"I sure hope Mr. Thompson didn't have any trouble loading her," Callie said as she gathered the rest of the tools and put them away.

Justin tested the stall door to make sure it latched properly. "Well, my dad's there to help him load up, and I'm sure Harvey'll volunteer to help. Besides," he said with a shrug, "she's small enough that someone could just pick her up and put her in the trailer."

"I can't wait until she gets here," Callie said. She ran over to her father and gave him a big hug.

"What was that for?" Mr. McLean asked.

"It's for a lot of things." Callie smiled. "But especially for understanding and helping so much with Moon Shadow."

Her father ruffled her hair and grinned. "Just don't make me sorry I had a weak moment."

Everyone laughed. They put out the rest of the fresh straw, then closed the stall door and went to wait in the driveway.

"There they are!" Callie's mother pointed to the big, blue truck that was just rounding the bend.

Celah whinnied when she saw the horse trailer and raced to the fence, her ears pricked, curious to see what was being delivered. Callie had to laugh when the big mare snorted at the sight of the tiny buckskin being unloaded.

"She's too little to even be near you right now, old girl," Callie said as she patted the big mare. "All you'd have to do is sidestep and Moon Shadow would be squished flat."

Callie heard a funny noise and turned in time to see a speckled brown goat tromping down the ramp behind Moon Shadow, its long ears flapping as it went.

"I thought it might come in handy to have your milk fresh on tap," Mr. Thompson said. "You can keep Matilda here until this filly is weaned."

Callie's father helped Mr. Thompson get Moon Shadow into her stall, and the goat into an outside corral. When the new arrivals were settled in, Mr. McLean shook Mr. Thompson's hand. "I really appreciate everything you've done for our daughter," he said.

"It was my pleasure." Mr. Thompson returned the firm grip. "That girl of yours does twice the work of my boy. I've got to keep her happy so she'll stay on working for the rest of the summer. The show season has started and Luke and Jill will be putting in a lot of time on their halter horses." He made a shooing motion to Callie. "You run along now and play with your new filly. I'll expect you over at the ranch bright and early tomorrow."

"Yes sir, Mr. Thompson," Callie said, giving him a snappy salute. "And thank you for everything!" She scrambled toward the barn to join her friends. "Isn't she beautiful?" she said to Billie as she squeezed between her and Justin and leaned her chin on the stall door.

"She's perfect," Billie said. "Can we go in and touch her?"

Justin opened the door, letting the girls walk in ahead of him. Moon Shadow seemed to be tired out from the short trip. She ignored the three people standing around looking at her and folded her front legs and collapsed in the sweet-smelling straw.

"She's going to need a feeding pretty soon," Justin said. "Come on, Callie, I'll show you how to milk that goat."

He exited the barn and came back a few minutes later leading the speckled goat with a halter. He dragged over several bales of hay and pushed them close together, then lifted the little goat on top of the hay. "She'll be easier to milk if she's up off the ground," he explained. Then he grabbed a small pan and showed Callie and Billie how to milk the goat. "It might be easier on both you and the goat if you collect enough milk at once to make several feedings. You can keep the extra in the refrigerator."

Billie ran her hand across Moon Shadow's silky coat. "She's so beautiful, and so soft." She turned to Callie. "Can I help you feed her?"

Justin handed the fresh pan of goat's milk to Callie. "Here you go. Her milk pail is in the corner."

Callie poured out a ration of milk into the bucket and handed it to Billie. "Let's get her up, then you can hold this for her while she drinks."

As soon as Moon Shadow saw her meal being delivered, she nickered and tried to stand, but her hindquarters collapsed under her. She had to make several more attempts before she successfully gained her feet.

"Wow, look at her go," Billie said in surprise as the filly began to gulp the milk. "It's almost gone already!"

When the milk was finished, Moon Shadow pulled her head from the bucket, dripping milk from the curly whiskers on her chin.

"Can we give her more?" Billie asked.

Justin took the empty bucket and dipped it into the water trough. He swirled the water to rinse off the sides, then dumped it out the door. "You need to be careful that you don't overfeed this filly," he warned. "Too much milk could make her sick."

A horn sounded outside the barn and Mrs. McLean called, "Billie, your father is here!"

"Shoot," Billie said. "I wish I didn't have to go. I'd rather stay and help you, Callie. I've never been around a foal this young before."

"Don't worry," Callie said with a chuckle. "I have to feed her every couple of hours for a while, so I'm going to need lots of help. You can come over any time you want, day or night!"

"My dad could drop me off on his way in to work for the next couple of days," Billie volunteered. I could stay here for a couple of hours and do some of the feedings while you're at work, then my mom could come get me at lunchtime."

Callie smiled in appreciation of her friend's offer. "That would help me and my parents out a lot."

❧

After a night of around-the-clock feedings, Callie dragged herself out of bed again so she could get Moon Shadow fed and all of her chores done before she left for work at the Thompson ranch.

She quickly milked the goat and fed Moon Shadow, leaving the extra milk in the fridge for Billie to feed the filly in her absence. Callie took a few extra minutes to work with her before she did her chores. Even though the tiny mustang was less than a week old, she needed to be handled several times a day so she'd become used to human touch.

Callie ran her hands over Moon Shadow's body and picked up her feet. The filly twitched and stomped her hind legs when she hit a ticklish spot. Callie had to be careful when lifting the filly's front feet. She'd discovered that Moon Shadow liked to play tricks. One of her favorites was nipping Callie on the pocket when she bent over to pick up a hoof.

When Callie finished, she let herself out of the stall and leaned on the door, observing the little buckskin as she shuffled around the stall on unsteady legs. The mustang found a spot in the center where the straw was deep and lay down in the straw.

It worried Callie that Moon Shadow didn't seem to be getting much stronger, despite the fact that she continued to have a good appetite. She decided to give Susan a call and have the vet give Moon Shadow a checkup.

"I'll be back in a few hours," Callie told the foal as she locked the stall door and went to the house. She left a message on Susan's cell phone, then fetched her bike. She pedaled down the road to the Thompson ranch, whistling a happy tune. The warm breeze blew through Callie's hair and she dreamed of the day when she'd be able to ride Moon Shadow across the open desert.

Jill was just pulling her prize yearling from the stall when Callie arrived. "Morning," Jill said, sounding almost businesslike. "You can start with Poco Queen's stall."

Callie nodded a hello. Jill seemed totally different than her goofball brother, Luke. Luke had dark hair, and Jill was a blonde. All Luke could think about was teasing and playing jokes on people, while Jill was super serious. Callie really admired her for being so dedicated, but in a way she was afraid of the older girl. She wished she wasn't so unapproachable.

Callie set her things down on a bale of hay and grabbed the wheelbarrow.

"Make sure you use three full bags of shavings to finish it off," Jill instructed. Then, with a small smile, she added, "Please."

The door at the far end of the barn banged open, and Luke came out of the barn's office with a cream puff in one hand and a maple bar in the other. "Hey, how's your mutt doing, Callie-o?" He smiled broadly, showing raspberry filling between his two front teeth.

Callie steered the wheelbarrow into the first stall, trying hard to ignore him. She knew he was just hoping to goad her into a fight. She picked up the muck rake and began to separate the good bedding from the bad, determined to forget that Luke was even there.

But the annoying boy wasn't about to let her off the hook that easily. He leaned on the door frame and popped the rest of the cream puff into his mouth. "So why'd you adopt a stupid mustang, anyway?" he asked.

Callie warned herself to keep cool. "Why not?"

Luke laughed and powdered sugar sprayed off his lips onto his clean shirt. "I can give you a hundred reasons *not* to buy a mustang, but it would take too long," he said. "My sister and I are practicing for our halter class this morning. Why don't you come out and see what a real horse can do?"

Callie paused with the muck rake in midair. She really wanted to throw some manure on the smarty-pants, but she knew Luke would run straight to his father and tattle on her. She went back to cleaning the stall, but the thought of watching a halter lesson did intrigue her. Maybe she could pick up a few pointers that would help her train Moon Shadow to lead.

Two hours later, she dumped the last load of manure and took a break. She grabbed a root beer from the refrigerator in the office and headed outside, squinting when she stepped into the glaring Nevada sun. It wasn't even ten o' clock and the temperature was already over eighty degrees. She put the ice-cold can of pop to her forehead, enjoying the coolness against her hot skin. Luke and Jill were in the small arena with their horses, so Callie found a shady spot beside the barn and sat down to watch what they were doing. One of the grooms, who Callie remembered was named José, came out for a break and stood beside her.

"Square your horse up, Luke," Mr. Thompson called from his spot in the arena fifty feet away.

Luke's dark bay colt was standing with his left hind leg six inches ahead of the other. But when Luke tried to fix the problem, the colt stepped forward, moving all four of his legs out of line.

"Try it again, son," Mr. Thompson said, then turned to his daughter. "Your filly looks good, Jill. Now walk her toward me on a straight line and stop ten feet away."

Callie watched as Jill did as she was told. Her filly was behaving perfectly, and Callie could tell that Jill must have done a lot more work with her horse than her brother had done with his. Jill stopped her filly ten feet from her father and made sure all of Poco Queen's legs were square. What puzzled Callie was that Jill moved to the other side of her horse while her father was inspecting it.

"Why is she doing that?" Callie asked José.

The older man smiled. "Mr. Thompson is acting as the show judge," he explained. "It's Jill's job to make sure she stays out of the way. If she gets between the judge and the horse, that could cost her points. When the judge finishes his inspection, Jill will move back to her horse's left side again."

"Maybe I could try that with my new foal," Callie said.

José gave a deep laugh and patted her on the head. "Miss Jill's been working with this filly for over a year. If you've got a brand-new foal in your barn, I think you'll find there are a few extra steps you'll need to do before you take that little horse to the show ring. These things take time, Callie." He walked away, shaking his head in amusement.

Callie frowned. She had no idea why José was laughing. But several hours later back in Moon Shadow's stall, she found out exactly why he'd found her comment so funny. She took down the new blue halter that Billie had given her and hooked it over Moon Shadow's petite head. Every time Callie tugged on the lead rope, Moon Shadow stubbornly pulled back, and one time she even tipped over backward. After battling the filly for several minutes, Callie sat in the straw and tried to catch her breath. To her dismay, Moon Shadow stepped forward and nuzzled her hair, then folded her front legs and plopped down beside her. Callie was glad the groom wasn't there to witness the fiasco.

"This isn't working," she said as she played with the filly's wispy black mane. "Maybe my parents will have some ideas." She sighed and rested her head against Moon Shadow's neck, breathing in the warm horse scent. It was the best smell ever.

A few minutes later, she heard her mother's voice from the barn door. "Are you in here, Callie?"

Callie stood up and waved. "Over here!"

Mrs. McLean peeked over the stall door. "Looks like you two have been taking a nap together." She let herself into the stall and quietly approached the filly.

Moon Shadow scrambled to her feet and bobbed her head, taking a couple of steps forward. Then she stopped and sniffed Mrs. McLean's clothes.

"Actually, we were both taking a rest," Callie told her mother. "Do you know anything about teaching a foal to lead? She doesn't want to walk on a lead rope."

"We had horses when I was growing up," Mrs. McLean said. "Moon Shadow's a little young. I wouldn't expect too much yet, but there's no reason you can't get her started." She went to retrieve a long rope that hung on the wall of the barn. "Hook this to one side of her halter, and run it around her hindquarters and back up to the other side of the halter." She showed Callie how to do it. "Now, when you give the rope a gentle tug, it will tighten around her haunches, making her think that something is pushing her from behind. She should step forward."

Callie gave the rope a pull. It startled Moon Shadow, causing her to jump forward several feet. She eased off on the pressure and tried again. This time the little mustang took several tentative steps forward. Callie patted her and told her what a good girl she was, then tried it again. Soon Moon Shadow was following her hesitantly around the stall. "She's walking on a lead rope!" Callie said excitedly.

Her mother clapped her hands in delight. "You'll probably have to keep that rope around her hindquarters for quite a while since she's so young," she said. "They're pretty stubborn for their first few months."

"You can say that again!" Callie laughed. "It's a good thing she makes up for it by being so lovable."

"Well, time for a break. I'm making us a late lunch," Mrs. McLean said. "Come on up to the house when you get the halter off that little filly."

Moon Shadow found her usual spot in the center of the stall and stretched out on her side. In no time at all, she seemed to be in a deep sleep. The filly looked as if she didn't have a care in the world.

But Callie couldn't relax until she'd heard what Dr. Susan had to say.

Fourteen

❦

The vet took out her stethoscope and listened to Moon Shadow's heart and lungs. Callie chewed her bottom lip and shredded several stems of hay while she waited. After several minutes of poking and prodding, Dr. Susan turned to Callie and her parents. "Everything appears to be in working order," she said. "This filly just seems to be a little weak. That's normal, considering that she was born a bit prematurely. She also didn't get all of the colostrum she needed at birth from her mother's milk."

"Colostrum is what the foals need in their first twenty-four hours to help them build their immune system so they don't get sick," Callie explained to her parents.

"You're getting to be quite the expert," Mr. McLean said. "I guess hanging around with the doc here has started to rub off a little." He gave a playful tug on Callie's shirt collar.

Callie beamed.

Susan let herself out of the stall. "Well, Callie has definitely been a big help," she said as she reached into her bag and pulled out a bottle of liquid vitamins and a syringe. "Now if I can just get her to hold this filly still for a moment, I'll give Moon

Shadow an injection that should sharpen her up a bit. I'll be back in a few days to check on her."

"Thanks, Susan," Mr. McLean said. "I've got to get back to my garden right now. Why don't you leave the bill with my wife, and we'll write you a check next week?"

Susan shook her head. "Callie's put in a lot of time with me lately, and she'll still be working weekends all summer. The vet care is on the house."

Mrs. McLean took Susan's free hand in both of hers. "You don't know how much this means to us," she said. "We truly thank you from the bottom of our hearts."

"I'm happy to do it," Susan said. "I consider it a fair trade." She winked at Callie, then administered the shot to Moon Shadow and packed up her gear to leave. "I'll see you next weekend if you're not too tired out from the feeding schedule and working at the Thompsons' place," Susan told her. "You're looking a little tired. Why don't you let your parents do the next feeding, and you go get some rest?"

Callie nodded and thanked the vet for her visit. She yawned as she waved good-bye. Susan was right. A nice nap sounded wonderful at the moment.

And now that she knew Moon Shadow would be okay, it would be a lot easier to sleep.

The next several weeks went by in a blur of work and late-night feedings. Billie's parents let her sleep over at Callie's house several times, and the two girls slept on hay bales in the barn and got up to feed Moon Shadow every two or three hours. Justin even came over on a few occasions to help out, and Callie's parents filled in the feed times when Callie was working and Billie couldn't be there.

Little by little, Moon Shadow started to gain strength. Her gaunt sides filled out and she even began to play and romp like a normal foal. Callie's father fenced off a small section of Celah's pen so the little mustang would have a place to play outside. The two horses spent lots of time nosing each other through the fence.

One day Harvey dropped by. When Moon Shadow walked up to the fence to greet him, he waved a fistful of timothy hay under her nose. Moon Shadow nibbled on the tops of the sweet grass stems.

Callie laughed when the filly lolled her tongue at first, trying to spit the hay out, but the little buckskin came right back and took another dainty bite. This time she chewed thoughtfully and reached for more.

"Does she have enough teeth to chew?" Callie asked, looking up at Harvey.

"She's already got a full set of back teeth to grind with," the mustanger explained. "It's the front ones that take a month or so to come in. I brought you a whole bale of that timothy hay. You should start giving this filly a little bit each day. It's time for her to start adding solid food to her diet. Once she's eating okay, you can ease up a little between your milk feedings."

"Thanks, Harvey," Callie said, giving him a big hug. "You've really been a huge help."

Harvey patted her on the head and looked slightly embarrassed by the display of affection, but Callie saw the way his eyes shone when he turned to go. Once again, she considered herself very lucky to have such good friends.

Callie waved good-bye to Harvey, then gathered Moon Shadow's halter and lead. "Guess what time it is," she called to her as she dangled the halter over the fence. Moon Shadow trotted up as if she were anxious to start her lessons, but, as usual, once the halter was on she showed just how stubborn she could be.

Over the next month and a half, Callie worked with Moon Shadow every day. The filly still got tired easily, but she was always up for pranks. One day Moon Shadow would walk on the end of the lead line perfectly, and Callie would take her all over the farm. Then the next day, Moon Shadow would come out of her stall standing on her hind legs and pawing the air.

Callie spent a lot of time and patience handling the little buckskin. Justin showed her how to pick up the filly's feet without causing her concern, and how to desensitize her ticklish spots like the ears and belly. Callie was surprised one afternoon when Justin brought in some white plastic garbage bags and started rubbing one of them across Moon Shadow's back. Justin explained that horses were easily frightened by moving objects, especially something blowing in the wind. "But if we expose her to things like this now while she's young," he told Callie, "when she's old enough for you to ride her, she'll be less likely to spook and dump you off when something blows by."

At first Moon Shadow objected when they rubbed the plastic bags, newspapers, and tarps over her back or shook beneath her belly. But as Callie and Justin spent time each day working on the lesson, the filly eventually became used to it.

Callie hadn't realized that raising a foal could be so much work. She knew she wouldn't be able to do it without the help of her willing friends.

Billie had never handled a foal before either, and she was thrilled to learn right along with Callie. Whenever Harvey or Justin volunteered time to teach them, the girls were eager to learn.

"Maybe one of these days I can breed Star and I'll have a foal of my own to raise," Billie said with a dreamy look in her eye.

"Let's just hope your foal won't be half as stubborn as Moon Shadow is," Callie said, pretending to frown as she pulled her shirttail out of the filly's clamped teeth.

The only thing that made her feel better about her slow progress with Moon Shadow was watching Luke work with his halter colt. On her good days, Callie's little mustang was better than Luke's spoiled bay.

Callie had gotten in the habit of spending her breaks watching Luke and Jill in the arena. The show ring drills Mr. Thompson made his kids practice fascinated her. She no longer hid in the shadows of the barn, but settled in a shady spot right by the arena fence. Jill never seemed to mind, but she knew it irritated Luke, especially when he was making a lot of mistakes. Callie just kept on watching. She considered it payback for all of the mean things he'd ever said to her.

One day while she was eating her peanut-butter-and-honey sandwich, Luke lost his patience and started jerking on his colt's halter. The well-muscled colt rose into the air, pulling the lead rope out of Luke's hands.

Callie threw down her sandwich and jumped up as the young colt raced across the side of the arena, his tail cocked over his back. She put out her hand. Luke's bay slowed down, slid to a stop, then circled back to see her. Callie quietly reached out and caught the bay, talking softly to calm him.

Luke stomped across the arena to retrieve his colt. "What are *you* smirking at?" he grouched, snatching the rope from her hand. "You think you and that puny yellow horse could do any better?"

Callie watched him go, imagining her and Moon Shadow standing in a halter class competition at a horse show, between Luke and his sister. One thing was for sure. On a good day, Moon Shadow *could* compete in a halter class with Luke's horse. On a good day, Moon Shadow had much better manners.

She finished her sandwich and went back to work. The last job she had to do before she could go home was cleaning the barn's office. She eyed all of the soda and juice cans lining the counter. It was too bad she couldn't just put the trash can at the end of the counter and swipe them all in with one big sweep of her arm, but there were other things on the counter, too.

As she picked up the trash, Callie set aside some of the show entry forms that lay on the counter. The bold headline on one of them caught her eye: End of Year All-Breeds Show. She quickly scanned the information, noting that there were several halter classes available. The arena was only a couple of roads over from her house. If she were to enter Moon Shadow in a show class, she'd be able to walk the filly to the arena.

Jill entered the tack room and Callie quickly put the entry form back on the counter, the heat of embarrassment rising in her cheeks. Feeling like a kid caught with her hand in the cookie jar, she fussed with the remaining cans and stacked the rest of the entry forms in a neat pile. Jill got a juice out of the refrigerator and took a long swig. As the tall, lanky girl headed back out of the tack room, she turned to Callie and said over her shoulder, "I can make a copy of that if you want." Then, without waiting for an answer, she breezed out the door. Callie stood dumbfounded. How did Jill know what she'd been thinking? Mr. Thompson had driven by their house many times when Justin had been out in the paddock helping her with Moon Shadow. Had Mr. Thompson told Jill about her fumbling attempts to school Moon Shadow?

Was it really possible that she could enter Moon Shadow in an All-Breeds Show?

Her excitement began to build as she pictured herself in a long-strided march, trotting alongside Moon Shadow as they went back and forth in front of the show judge and then stood in the lineup with the other colts and fillies being judged on their confirmation and manners.

Moon Shadow looked great now. Her coat was slick and shiny and her fuzzy mane had grown long enough to lie down like it was supposed to. But would people laugh at her for entering a mustang in a show with registered horses?

A wave of shame passed over Callie. All of this time, she had been criticizing others for thinking that mustangs weren't as good as other horses, and here she was having her own doubts. But were they really about Moon Shadow? Or was she simply afraid that she couldn't compete with Luke and Jill? So far, she'd only been *watching* their lessons. They were the ones who had actually been doing the work. Justin had been helping her school Moon Shadow for manners, but she'd never actually taken a real lesson on how to show a horse at halter.

After she made sure no one was outside the tack room, Callie picked up the entry form again and studied the available classes. There was one class for kids ages twelve to sixteen. It was possible that Luke and Jill might choose to enter another class. But what difference did it make? She knew she couldn't compete with their years of lessons, but she could still enter just for the experience. What was that old saying her dad was always repeating? *When the going gets tough, the tough get going!*

Callie stood up straight and squared her shoulders. Who cared if Moon Shadow wasn't a papered horse, or that she, Callie McLean, hadn't had years of expensive lessons? She had just as much right to walk into that show ring as Luke and Jill did. It would be fun, even if she took last place. At least she could say she had done it!

She finished up in the tack room and prepared to go home for the day. She'd ask her parents about entering the show. If they said yes, then maybe she'd get up the nerve to ask Jill for a copy of the entry form.

There was no one around but José when Callie left. She said good-bye, then picked up her bike and pedaled down the road to her house.

She felt pretty proud of herself for making the decision to gather her courage and step into the show ring with Moon Shadow. But just as she got herself pumped up, she was hit by another thought: the twenty-dollar entry fee for the show. Even if she could overcome that obstacle, she had neither a show halter nor special show clothes.

Callie frowned in frustration. A show halter with all of its fancy silver trim and the elegant outfits that competitors wore would cost way more than she could afford.

She pulled into the driveway of her house, propped her bike against the porch steps, and headed straight to the barn to feed Moon Shadow. She filled the milk bucket and took it out to the paddock where the filly was sleeping next to the fence in the shadow cast by the draft mare. The mustang woke with a start and scrambled to her feet, nickering greedily for her lunch. Callie smiled when she saw Moon Shadow's strong, steady walk. The little mustang was still smaller than most horses her age, but she'd come a long way from the weak little foal that had stumbled out of the horse trailer just a few short months ago.

Callie ran her fingers through the filly's black mane while the little one slurped noisily at the milk. "We almost got a chance to prove ourselves to all those people who doubted us," she told her, feeling tears spring up behind her eyes. "But I guess we'll have to wait until next summer. Maybe by then I'll be able to save enough to buy me a decent show outfit and you the best show halter I can find."

Moon Shadow had made so much progress in such a short period of time, Callie thought. It was a shame that she wouldn't be able to show off the results of all of their hard work this summer. For now, she'd have to content herself with showing off in her own pasture for Billie and Justin.

Fifteen

❧

Just before sunset Callie went out to put Moon Shadow in her stall. "Susan says we can wean you off all the milk in another week," she said as she tossed a flake of grass hay into the feeder her father had installed a few weeks ago. Moon Shadow grabbed a big bite of hay and blew through her lips.

Callie laughed. "I guess that means you don't think too much of that idea," she said, taking off her watch and pouring some water into the milk bucket to wash it out. She was just getting ready to go back in the house when she heard a noise at the barn door. She almost fell over with surprise when Luke Thompson removed his hat and stepped into the barn.

"So this is the famous mustang," he said.

"What do you want, Luke?" Callie crossed her arms and watched him saunter across the barn to Moon Shadow's stall.

"I just wanted to come by and take a look at this horse you've been jaw-jacking about all summer." He picked up a stem of hay and put it between his teeth, then leaned on the stall door.

"This is Moon Shadow," Callie said proudly. "She might not have come from a long fancy line of registered horses like your colt, but I love her anyway."

"She's pretty nice for a mustang," Luke admitted as he opened her stall door and let himself in uninvited.

Callie watched Luke walk around the stall, inspecting her filly in the waning light.

"Not bad." He stood there with his hands in his pockets, watching Moon Shadow eat.

"What is it you want?" Callie said again.

Luke put his hands in the air. "Come on, Callie, I didn't do anything to make you so huffy. Why do you always act so prickly when I'm around? Can't we agree to a truce?"

Callie sighed. Outside of showing up uninvited, he hadn't really done anything wrong. "Come on out of the stall," she said, walking toward the barn door. "It's getting late, and I'm sure you want to get home before dark." She led the way back out to the driveway. "Okay, Luke," she added, attempting a smile. "I'll try not to be so grouchy when you're around."

Luke plopped his hat back on his head and grinned. "That's better. You know, you're a whole lot prettier when you smile, Callie McLean."

Great, Callie thought. *That was all I needed—Luke Thompson thinking I'm pretty.* The compliment would go a whole lot further if it came from Justin.

Her cheeks immediately grew warm. Why had she thought of something crazy like that?

Luke pulled something out of his back pocket and handed it to her.

"What's this?" Callie asked.

"Jill said to bring it to you, but I don't know what you'd want with a show entry." He saw the irritated look on Callie's face and backed up a step. "Oops, sorry. I forgot about our truce." He headed down the driveway and climbed on his ATV. "Jill said to give that to you, and I did. So I'm out of here." With that he started the engine and drove off in a cloud of dust.

Callie shook her head. She'd never understand boys if she lived to be a hundred. She looked down at the entry form in her hands. It was nice of Jill to think of her, but there was no way she'd be able to use the entry form this year.

A soft breeze blew the smoky aroma of barbequed hamburgers from the back porch. It was almost dinnertime. She looked at her wrist and remembered that she'd left her watch by Moon Shadow's stall. Callie stuck the entry form in her back pocket as she walked toward the barn. She expected the usually friendly nicker when she flipped on the barn light, but instead she was greeted by silence.

"Hey, girl, are you lying down already?" Callie said, approaching the stall. But she stopped dead at the sight of the unlatched stall door. "No!" Callie cried. She ran to the stall, not believing her eyes. Why hadn't she checked the latch when Luke left the stall? Mr. Thompson had said his son was careless about locking gates and stall doors.

She turned in a frantic circle, hoping that Moon Shadow had only wandered to a corner of the barn, but the filly was nowhere in sight.

Callie grabbed the blue halter and lead rope and ran out the door. "Shadow!" she hollered as she ran around to Celah's corral to see if the filly was there. Celah was prancing up and down the fence line and snorting. "Where is she, girl?" Callie wailed.

Celah stared off into the desert and called to the runaway filly, her sides shaking with the force of her neigh.

Callie's parents came running. "What's going on here?" her mother asked.

Callie felt a sob rising in her throat. "Moon Shadow got loose." The full moon was coming up and she strained to see in the gathering darkness.

"How did this happen?" Mr. McLean asked.

Callie brushed angrily at a tear that slipped down her cheek. "Luke came to deliver something and he went into the stall with Moon Shadow," she explained. "And I was in such a hurry to get rid of him that I forgot to check the lock." She balled her fists at her sides. "I was so stupid! I should have checked the lock."

"Okay, honey," her mother said. "Now is not the time to lay blame. First we have to find your horse. Let's split up. You stay close to the house, Callie, in case she comes back. Your father and I will go looking for her."

Callie pointed toward the hills to the east where the full moon was rising. "Celah was staring in that direction. I'm sure that's where Moon Shadow went."

"I'll go that way," said Mr. McLean. He picked up a coil of rope and an extra halter. "Sara, you head in the opposite direction, and Callie, stay here," he said. "I don't want you getting lost, too." He took off at a jog, heading into the hills.

How can they expect me to just wait at home? Callie wondered as she paced behind the barn, straining to hear anything that would indicate that Moon Shadow was out there. The full moon was rising higher and she could see the outline of the sagebrush and a scattering of trees on the distant hills.

Celah whinnied again and Callie thought she heard an answering call. She held perfectly still, refusing to breathe as she listened to the sounds of the night.

There! She heard it again—the sound of a scared whinny in the distance. Callie couldn't stand it anymore. She knew her parents would probably ground her, but she had to disobey them in this case. Moon Shadow was in danger!

She picked up the halter where she'd tossed it on the ground and took off in the direction of Moon Shadow's last call. Callie ran as fast as she could. When she reached the open desert, she stopped to get her bearings. She knew these trails. She'd ridden them hundreds of times in the last couple of years. She chose the trail that led to the spot where she'd witnessed the mustang battle at the beginning of the summer. If she didn't find her filly before she reached the outcrop, at least she'd be able to stand on the high rocks and look out over the entire area.

"Shadow!" Callie called. "Here, girl." She walked for another ten minutes, listening to the night sounds of the desert. A chill went up her spine when a coyote howled in the distance. Several more coyotes joined in the cry, and Callie quickened her pace. She had to find Moon Shadow—and fast.

Callie picked her way among the desert brush. She stumbled several times when she wandered off the trail and tripped over a low-lying branch or a partially buried rock. A loud snap sounded to her right and Callie stopped in her tracks, the hair on the back of her neck standing on end.

"Moon Shadow?" she called softly into the night. "Mom, Dad?" How far away were those coyotes? Callie wondered. She racked her brain, trying to remember if she'd ever heard of a coyote attacking a human. "Is...is someone there?" Her voice shook and she rubbed her arms to rid herself of the goose bumps that had popped up there.

There was a sudden snapping of branches and Callie's heart dropped into her shoes. She opened her mouth to scream, but the loud snort of a horse stopped her. Then a dark shape materialized out of the darkness.

"Moon Shadow!" Callie hollered as the little buckskin raced toward her, her golden coat shimmering in the light of the moon.

Moon Shadow cocked her tail over her back and raced past Callie, her head held high as she enjoyed her freedom.

Callie sucked in her breath, marveling at the beauty of the mustang foal as she galloped down the trail with her mane and tail flying, jumping the sage and bitterbrush that got in her way.

"Shadow, come here, girl," she called as the filly turned and made another pass. Callie put out her hand and beckoned to her. Moon Shadow made several more wild canters to and fro, then pulled down to a high-stepping trot. The filly circled Callie as she stood with her hand outstretched.

Moon Shadow halted and raised her head high, blowing loudly through her nose in a powerful snort.

"Now you're just being a show-off," Callie scolded. She approached slowly and buckled the halter over the filly's head. Moon Shadow nuzzled her shoulder and Callie threw her arms around her neck, breathing a huge sigh of relief. "I thought you were gone," she whispered into the mustang's sweat-dampened coat.

Moon Shadow blew through her lips and tossed her head.

"Are you ready to go back to your stall?" Callie led the way back down the trail and Moon Shadow followed eagerly.

When they reached the barn, both of her parents were waiting anxiously with all of the outdoor lights turned on. "Callie?" her mother's voice cut through the night.

"I'm here, Mom and Dad," Callie called out. "I found Moon Shadow." She stepped into the circle of light. Her father took the filly from her while her mother folded her in a big embrace.

"If I wasn't so happy to see the two of you, I'd ground you for the rest of your life!" Mrs. McLean said. "I thought we told you to stick near the house."

Callie hung her head. "I'm really sorry, Mom. I just couldn't stand the thought of Moon Shadow being out there all by herself—especially when I heard the coyotes howling."

"Coyotes? Well, how do you think we felt about *you* being out there all alone?" her father said sternly.

Callie nodded. She was in big trouble.

"You're going to have to do some extra time in the garden for disobeying," Mrs. McLean said. "And you can spend the rest of the evening in your room. Your father and I will take care of Moon Shadow tonight. Get going," she said as she shooed Callie toward the house.

Callie slowly made her way to her bedroom. Moon Shadow was safe. That was all that mattered. She'd gladly accept any punishment her parents gave her.

Sixteen

❧

allie slept soundly knowing that Moon Shadow was safely tucked away in her stall and her parents were watching over her. When the sun came up the next morning, she bounded out of bed and quickly changed her clothes. She had forty-five minutes to do her chores and check in on Moon Shadow before she left for the ranch. As she pulled on her boots, she noticed that her parents had already moved her filly out front to the paddock next to Celah's.

"Good morning," her mother said as she rounded the corner of the barn. "Moon Shadow has already been fed, but you can finish her stall before you leave for the Thompsons'."

Callie quickly completed her chores, then picked up a soft brush and spent a few extra minutes grooming her filly and Celah. Star nickered from her pen and Callie slipped the mare a piece of carrot. "Your mom will be here this afternoon," she said as she rubbed the chestnut's neck. "I'm almost out of time. You'll have to wait for Billie to brush you."

She finished with Celah and moved on to Moon Shadow. She groomed the filly until the dapples stood out on her shining coat. It really was too bad that she couldn't enter her filly in that end-of-year show. But next show season she'd be ready for sure.

She put the brushes away and headed for the house. Her mother met her at the kitchen door and handed her an apple and a raisin bagel. "Don't forget you've got some weeding to do when you get home," she said with a lift of her eyebrow.

Callie nodded as she stuffed the bagel in her shirt pocket and took a big bite of the apple. The juice ran down her chin and she wiped it with her sleeve. She grabbed her bike from the side of the house and pedaled to the Thompson ranch.

"Good morning," Mr. Thompson greeted Callie as she walked into the barn and took the muck rake down from its nail on the wall. "I hear you're going to be entering the last show of the season."

Callie shook her head. "Maybe next year." She took the wheelbarrow from its spot and rolled it to the first stall.

"Why are you waiting?" Mr. Thompson asked.

Callie shrugged. "I can't enter," she said. "I don't have a show halter, or any fancy clothes to wear for the competition."

"I see," Mr. Thompson said. "Excuse me just a minute." He walked toward the office and returned a moment later. "This might be a little big, but I'm sure you could punch an extra hole in it." He handed her a black leather show halter with silverwork running down the cheek band and across the nosepiece. "Return it to me when you're finished."

Callie's mouth dropped open. She reached for the halter and ran her fingers over the ornate silver designs. "Oh, Mr. Thompson, it's beautiful! The color will be perfect for Moon Shadow."

Mr. Thompson smiled. "Go on up to the house when you're done here. I believe my wife has kept all of the old show clothes that Jill's outgrown. I'll ask her to help you pick out something for the show." He handed her the lead that matched the halter. "I've seen you watching the kids' lessons, so I know you've learned what you've got to do."

Callie nodded. "I know Moon Shadow and I don't stand a chance at winning—especially if we're in the same class with Luke or Jill—but I think it'll be fun."

Mr. Thompson ruffled her hair. "That's the right spirit," he said. "Both Luke and Jill like to enter that class, but don't worry. It's your first show. You need to go in there with a positive attitude and show your fine little horse to the best of both of your abilities."

"I've been practicing with Moon Shadow, but she's kind of feisty," Callie said. "Sometimes she just wants to play."

"Your best bet would be to work with her every day between now and the show. If you can, take her someplace where there are a lot of people and noise," Mr. Thompson suggested. "That's mostly what upsets a new horse. She's used to going through her paces at home where everything is quiet. Then when you take her out among the crowds and confusion, you can't expect her not to be distracted."

"I'll do that. Thanks, Mr. Thompson, for everything!"

Callie whistled while she finished her work. She and Moon Shadow were going to the show!

Billie was waiting for Callie when she returned home from the ranch. "What've you got there?" Billie asked as she took the clothing from Callie's arms and inspected it. "Wow, that's pretty fancy stuff. It looks like a western show outfit."

Callie grinned as she held up the halter. "The Thompsons loaned me a halter and some clothes so I could enter Moon Shadow in the show at the end of the month."

"A show? That is so cool!" Billie said. "Can I help?"

Callie motioned for her friend to follow her into the house. "For starters, you can help me convince my parents that this is a good idea." She told her about Moon Shadow's escape the night before.

"Do you think Luke left the stall unlatched on purpose?" Billie asked. "I wouldn't put it past him."

"I don't think so. He's always been pretty bad about closing gates and locking stuff." Callie kicked off her boots and opened the back door of the house. "But you never know about that guy."

Callie found her mother in the sewing room. She carefully laid the clothing out on a chair. "I know I'm in trouble for disobeying you last night, Mom, but I have a favor to ask," she said. At her mother's nod, she continued, "There's a show at the end of the month and I'd like to enter Moon Shadow in the halter class. It doesn't cost much, anyway, and I've already got the money saved."

Mrs. McLean inspected the shiny material of the western show vest, poking at a rip in the seam. "Where did you get these?" she asked.

"The Thompsons loaned me the clothing and a show halter," Callie said as she showed her mother the beautiful black and silver halter. "I promised them I'd take really good care of all this stuff."

Her mother held up the white long-sleeved shirt and black pants, measuring them with her eyes to see if they would fit

Callie. "Are you sure you and Moon Shadow are up to this?" she asked. "You don't have any experience in showing, honey."

Callie shoved her hands into her pockets. "I've been watching Jill and Luke work with their halter horses all summer," she said. "And I've practiced a lot with Moon Shadow. The show is just down the road. We can walk there."

Billie cut in. "I'll help Callie any way I can. She's been working really hard. I know she and Moon Shadow can do this."

Mrs. McLean considered the idea. "Well, outside of that little slip-up we had with Moon Shadow last night, you've been a pretty good kid this summer. I'll have to talk with your father. If it's all right with him, then it's fine with me. I'll have to fix this vest, though."

Callie gave her mother a big hug. "Thanks, Mom. You're the best!"

The following two weeks went by in a total blur. Every minute of Callie's days was filled with working at the ranch, doing her own chores, practicing for the horse show, and helping Dr. Susan on weekends. She had to get up at dawn every morning just to get everything done.

Moon Shadow was growing rapidly, and was now on a total diet of hay and grain. All of the work that Callie had been doing with her had developed the filly's muscles. When she walked Moon Shadow down the road, neighbors always commented on how beautiful the little mustang was.

Callie worked hard on the lessons she had learned watching the Thompson kids. Billie came out a lot to help, and Justin rode his gelding over from the mustang pens as often as he could. With all of the extra help, Moon Shadow was definitely making progress. Callie knew they were far behind the other kids who had been showing all summer, but the young mustang had fallen into the routine and was behaving in a respectable manner.

One day Callie overheard Luke talking about a baseball game with his friends. She decided to take Moon Shadow. That would be the perfect place to follow up on Mr. Thompson's advice and expose her horse to the bustle and noise of a crowd. Billie saddled up Star so Moon Shadow would have some moral support, and just before the game was to begin, they walked the horses over to the local park.

There weren't a lot of people, but the kids in the game and the dozen or so onlookers made enough commotion to startle the filly and give her a good dose of what she'd encounter at the busy show grounds. Luke was the loudest of the bunch. Every time he hit a home run, he made sure the entire neighborhood heard about it.

In the beginning, Moon Shadow snorted and bolted about when she heard the cheering of the crowd. Once she gave Callie a good scare when she almost broke loose from her hold. But after a while, when she saw that Star wasn't bothered, Moon Shadow learned to ignore the noise and all the people running around. She became more concerned with outmaneuvering Star for the small dried tufts of bunchgrass that grew in the sandy desert soil outside the baseball diamond.

"I think she's ready," Billie said as she tugged Star away from the grass and they headed back to Callie's house. "Just two more days, and we'll be at the show!"

Callie swallowed hard. Where had the time gone? "Don't

expect any miracles," she warned her friend. "Right now I'm just hoping to get through this in one piece."

Billie reached out and booted her with the toe of her riding boot. "Don't talk like that, Cal. You'll be fine."

Callie pressed her lips in a thin line. She knew her friend was right. She really shouldn't worry.

But when the morning of the show finally arrived, Callie woke with butterflies in her stomach. Her hands shook when she pulled on her old work clothes and boots.

"You're up awfully early," Mrs. McLean said when Callie cut through the kitchen on her way to the back door. "Not so fast," her mother added, pointing to the bowl of granola on the table.

Callie held her stomach. "I can't eat a single bite, Mom."

Mrs. McLean handed her a piece of toast and an orange. "Toast is always good for an upset stomach. You can eat the orange later when you aren't so nervous."

"Thanks, Mom," Callie said, grabbing the simple breakfast and bolting out the door. Her father was already at the barn when she arrived.

"I drew a couple of buckets of warm water," he said, pointing to the corner of the barn. "That light yellow filly picks up every speck of dirt she comes across, and she's already had a good roll this morning."

Callie tied a hay net to the hitching post so Moon Shadow could eat while she gave her a bath. She scrubbed and rinsed the filly, then toweled her dry. "You're going to stay tied up so you don't roll," she told Moon Shadow. "You've got to stay totally spotless until after our performance."

She packed a grooming kit to take to the show and placed it

in the backseat of the car. Her parents would drive over and meet her and Billie at the arena. When she was sure she'd packed everything she would need, she went to the house to collect her show clothes. Her mother had her outfit pressed and hanging on her bedroom door, but instead of Jill's old green western show vest, there was a sparkly bright blue vest in its place. "Mom?"

Mrs. McLean poked her head through the open door, smiling. "You've worked so hard with that filly, I figured you needed a really fancy outfit to show off a little to the other competitors."

"But I never even saw you working on it," Callie said, running her hand over the sparkles.

Her mother shrugged. "I stay up a lot later than you do."

Callie ran to her mother and hugged her. "Thanks, Mom," she whispered. "It's beautiful."

Mrs. McLean kissed the top of her daughter's head. "Your father and I are really proud of you and what you've done with Moon Shadow," she said. "When you walk into that show ring today, don't worry about anyone else or their big-deal horses. If you do your very best, you can hold your head up high and be proud of yourself. We're backing you one hundred percent!"

Callie nodded, feeling her throat tighten. It didn't matter that her family lived in a tiny house or that her parents were different from most. They loved and supported her, and she wouldn't trade them for anything!

"You'd better get ready," her mother said. "Billie will be here any minute now. You two go on ahead, and your father and I will meet you there with your outfit."

Together Callie and Billie walked Moon Shadow down the road to the show arena.

"Wow," Billie said when they entered the grounds, "I had no idea there would be this many people here."

Callie fought the butterflies taking flight in her stomach again. "I guess it's so crowded because it's an All-Breeds show," she said. "Any breed can enter any class. And that's a good thing, or I wouldn't be able to show Moon Shadow here today." She wondered how many competitors would be in her class.

They found a hitching post at the back of the lot near where all the trailers were parked and tied the horse to it. "Could you wait here with Moon Shadow while I go change my clothes and get my competition number?" Callie asked.

Billie nodded. "Here come your parents now. I'll hang the hay net so Moon Shadow will have something to keep her occupied. She's been pretty mellow so far, but we don't want her acting up."

Callie changed quickly in the backseat of her parents' car. The outfit was perfect—especially the new vest that her mother had sewn for her. She pulled on her polished boots and ran to the show office. Her class would be one of the first ones in the ring. She didn't have much time. As she stepped into the registration office, several heads turned to look at her. She recognized a couple of kids from her school. They smiled and waved at her and she returned the gesture, but she frowned when she saw Luke watching her from the corner.

"What're *you* doing here?" he said.

The comment took Callie by surprise. "You were the one who gave me the show entry form, remember?"

"Yeah," Luke scoffed, "but I didn't think you'd use it. Who in their right mind would enter a mustang in a show with registered stock?"

Callie refused to let Luke know that his comments hurt her. "I'm in the twelve-to-sixteen halter class," she said, forcing a smile.

He laughed in disbelief. "Yeah, right. Sure you are."

But when Callie picked up her number and headed out the door, she noticed that he wasn't laughing any more.

When Callie got back to Billie and Moon Shadow, the little mustang was standing quietly, eating her hay. Callie pulled her old shirt on over her new outfit to keep it from getting dirty, and ran a quick brush over the filly's coat. She followed up with a clean towel to get the last specks of dust. "Can you wait with Moon Shadow one more time?" she asked Billie. "I need to go wet this towel so I can wash off her muzzle before we go into the arena."

"Okay, but hurry. Your parents already went to find a seat in the bleachers. I think Justin's with them."

Knowing that Justin would be in the stands watching didn't do anything to calm Callie's nerves. She ran to the washroom and took several deep, calming breaths while she held the towel under the faucet.

The door opened and Jill Thompson stepped into the room. "Wow, you really *are* competing today," she said, surveying Callie from head to toe. "Your outfit looks great. I love that vest!"

Callie felt a little uneasy standing in the middle of the washroom, wearing clothing that used to belong to Jill. She wrung the excess water out of the towel. "Thanks," she said. "The pants and shirt are yours."

"Yeah, I recognized them," Jill said. "My mom told me you'd borrowed them. I hope they'll be as lucky for you as they were for me."

"You're not mad?" Callie said hesitantly.

Jill shook her head. "Why would I be mad? If you hadn't been cleaning stalls this summer, I wouldn't have had nearly as much time to spend with Poco Queen." She gave Callie a big grin. "Hey, I'm not worried about having a little competition. But Luke might be in trouble if you do well today." She scrutinized her image in the mirror. Apparently satisfied, she turned to go. "Good luck. I'll see you out there."

Callie stood alone in the washroom for a moment, surprised by the conversation that had just taken place. Jill usually seemed so unapproachable, but today she had actually been friendly. She'd even wished her luck.

The door opened again and Billie rushed in.

"Hey, what're you doing here?" Callie said. "I thought you were waiting with Moon Shadow."

Billie looked confused. "Luke told me you needed me."

Callie frowned. "I didn't tell him that."

What was going on? Luke Thompson was up to no good, and she was one hundred percent sure it involved Moon Shadow.

Seventeen

❧

As Callie and Billie hurried back to the hitching post
where they'd left Moon Shadow, they saw a commotion
up ahead.

"*Loose horse!*" someone yelled.

Callie's heart did a double flop when she spotted Moon
Shadow racing at breakneck speed across the parking lot with
her leather lead shank flying behind her. "Moon Shadow!" she
hollered at the top of her lungs. "Whoa!"

Callie gasped as the buckskin filly dodged to avoid a truck
that was just pulling onto the property. The little mustang's feet
went out from under her and she slid on her side for several
yards, then quickly scrambled to her feet.

Justin came running out of the stands and pushed his way
through the crowd of onlookers. "Whoa," he crooned as he
grabbed Moon Shadow's lead rope and tried to quiet her. "Easy
girl."

Callie and Billie ran as fast as they could. "I'm...so sorry,"
Billie said between gasps of breath.

"It's not your fault," Callie said.

As soon as she reached Justin and Moon Shadow, Callie stepped next to her filly and ran her hand over her neck. She could feel Moon Shadow's muscles quaking under her palm.

Jill was standing in the crowd with her chestnut filly. "What happened?" she asked as she tugged on Poco Queen's lead rope, trying to calm her down.

"I don't know," Callie said. She quickly inspected Moon Shadow for cuts and bruises while Justin held the filly. She brushed the dirt from the mustang's coat, frowning at all the brown stains she had gathered in the fall. "Your brother told Billie that I needed her, but I didn't. When we came out of the washroom, Moon Shadow was running down the parking lot like a maniac."

"I'm really sorry, Callie." Jill thought for a moment, then handed Poco Queen to a dark-haired girl next to her. "Luke was pretty upset when he found out you were in the show. I bet he's behind this for sure." She scanned the crowd. "I'll go tell my dad. He'll make Luke pull himself out of every class he entered."

"No, wait!" Callie said. "Thanks, Jill, but it's okay. We don't have any proof that he let Moon Shadow go on purpose."

The speaker system crackled and the announcer gave the five-minute call for the next class. Callie felt the sting of defeat. There was no way she could get Moon Shadow back to the other side of the parking lot and have her cleaned up in time. Tears pricked the backs of her eyelids. "I guess I'll be the one who pulls out of the class."

"No you won't," Jill said in a determined tone. "I've got a spot cleaner right here in my bag that'll take that dirt right out of your filly's coat."

While Justin held Moon Shadow, the three girls worked quickly, bathing the dirty parts, then towel-drying the filly's coat and brushing her repeatedly. With the sun shining warmly, Moon Shadow was clean and dry by the time the announcer gave the call to the gate.

"I don't know how to thank you," Callie said.

Jill winked. "Just do your best to beat my little brother, okay?"

Callie laughed and followed Jill into the show ring, mimicking everything the experienced competitor did. Fortunately, the run across the parking lot seemed to have burned up Moon Shadow's extra energy. She behaved perfectly as she stood between an Appaloosa filly and a black Morgan colt.

That was more than Callie could say for Luke's colt. The bay tossed his head and refused to stand still in the lineup. The competitors on either side of him had to move their horses away to give him more room.

As she waited to be called, Callie looked around the arena. The stands were pretty full. She searched the crowd for her parents and finally spotted them when Justin stood and waved his hat hollering, "Go get 'em, Callie!"

The crowd tittered with friendly laughter and Callie felt the heat rising in her cheeks. Her hands began to shake again as she became conscious of so many people watching her. What if she messed up and forgot what she was supposed to do?

The sun was beating down on the arena and Callie could feel the sweat trickling down her back. Her arms twitched nervously while she waited for the judge to call her forward. When the judge finally motioned that it was her turn, she thought she might pass out from sheer anxiety.

"Here we go, girl," Callie whispered to Moon Shadow. She took several deep breaths and asked her filly to walk the straight line to the judge. Her hand began to shake and Moon Shadow bobbed her head, signaling to Callie that she was transmitting her nervousness to her horse.

"How are you today?" the judge asked, giving her a pleasant smile.

Callie was taken completely by surprise. She hadn't expected the judge to actually *talk* to her.

"Fine," she managed to squeak.

The judge moved to the side of the horse and Callie gathered her wits enough to remember to get out of his way. She felt like a robot as she went through the moves, doing her best to show Moon Shadow off to her fullest.

"Relax," the judge said as he took his place at the head of her horse. "Remember, this is supposed to be fun," he added in a whisper, giving Callie a wink.

Callie tried hard to take his advice, but when the judge told her to trot back to the line, she was sure her knees were going to buckle. It took every ounce of courage she had to get back to where the others waited. Moon Shadow seemed to be enjoying herself, though. The little filly even cocked her tail over her back as they trotted back to the line. The crowd burst into applause.

Jill leaned forward from her place several horses away and mouthed the words, "You did great."

Callie tried to smile, but her top lip got stuck on her teeth. She could hear Jill giggling down the way.

As Callie stood and waited for everyone else to finish, her

breathing returned to normal and she even started to laugh at herself for being so silly. It was a good thing, too, because she needed to be smiling when the judge came by for his final inspection and the backing of all the horses.

When the man finally reached her, Callie put a little pressure on the lead rope and asked Moon Shadow to back up. The filly hesitated for just a second, then dutifully stepped backward. Callie smiled as she heard the crowd applaud, and the judge moved quickly on to the next contestant.

He finally raised his clipboard, indicating that he was through with the class, and Callie gave a big sigh of relief. She knew that Moon Shadow had done herself proud, but it was a tough competition. Jill and Poco Queen were a cinch to win. They hadn't made a single wrong move.

Callie patted Moon Shadow and straightened her halter. The chance of winning a ribbon in this experienced class of twelve horses was a long shot, but Callie was happy knowing that they'd both done their best.

"Here are your winners of Class Number Three," a woman's voice boomed over the loudspeaker. "In first place, it's number two-zero-six, Jill Thompson and Poco Queen!"

Callie gave Jill the thumbs-up sign and clapped loudly as the girl went forward to accept her ribbon.

A tall red-roan gelding won second place, and a boy she recognized from her school took third. Callie knew the class would award five ribbons. The owner of the beautiful palomino quarter horse next to her would probably take the next place. She looked down the row and saw Luke fidgeting with his colt. Callie didn't think Luke had performed very well, but from the look on his face, it was clear that he had expected to be called before now.

The announcer gave the next place and Callie clapped happily for the pretty palomino. She stared at Luke again. The boy looked totally shocked that he hadn't yet been called for a ribbon. If Luke didn't place, Callie promised herself that she would be sure to avoid him for at least a week. As rotten as the boy already was, his teasing and insults would be even worse after a defeat in the show ring.

The announcer called the last horse and Callie waited for Luke to step forward. Instead, he frowned and kicked at the dirt beneath his boots. Apparently, it wasn't his number they had called.

The boy standing next to her poked her in the shoulder. "Hey, aren't you number two-twenty-two? You just got the fifth-place ribbon. Congratulations!"

"Yeah, Callie! Way to go!" Her parents and Billie were yelling from the stands. Justin stood on the bench and whistled while he waved his cowboy hat.

Callie couldn't believe her ears. She even looked at the number pinned to her shirt to make sure the boy was right. The crowd laughed and applauded as the announcer called her number again, and Callie stepped forward with Moon Shadow prancing at her side.

"Congratulations!" said a pleasant-faced woman as she hooked the fifth-place ribbon on Moon Shadow's halter.

Callie asked her filly for a trot and they exited the arena with Moon Shadow bowing her neck and showing off for the crowd. Her parents and friends were waiting for her outside of the gate.

"You were awesome!" Billie said as she slapped Callie a high-five.

Justin pointed at her ribbon and gave her the thumbs-up sign. "I knew it all the time," he said.

"We're so proud of you, Callie," her mother and father said as they stepped forward to give her a big hug. Behind them, Dr. Susan waved.

Callie rubbed Moon Shadow's neck. "This little horse deserves all the credit," she said.

"No way," a voice said, and the crowd parted to let Jill Thompson through. "You deserve a lot of credit, too. And don't forget all those *free lessons* you got this summer from a pro," she added with a grin.

Callie grinned back. "Well, if you hadn't helped me get Moon Shadow cleaned up in time, I would never have made the class."

Jill shrugged. "No big deal. Listen, I've got to go, but, why don't you and Billie come to our 4-H meeting on Wednesday night? We could use a couple more girls with good horses." She waved and led her horse back to the trailer.

Callie smiled so broadly her cheeks hurt. With the help of her friends and family, all the hard work had definitely paid off. She and her beautiful yellow mustang had proved that it didn't take a long pedigree and lots of money to be a winner. They had done it all with patience and love. She gave Moon Shadow another pat.

"Just think what we'll have to show them next season, girl!"

About the Author

CHRIS PLATT has been riding horses since she was two years old. At the age of sixteen, she earned her first gallop license at a race-track in Salem, Oregon. Several years later, she became one of the first women jockeys in that state. Chris's other horse-related occupations have included training Arabian endurance horses and driving draft horses.

After earning a journalism degree from the University of Nevada in Reno, she decided to combine her love of horses with her writing. Her previous books include the Golden Heart Award–winning horse novel WILLOW KING, its sequel RACE THE WIND, and many others in the popular *Thoroughbred* series.

Chris lives in Nevada with her husband, six horses, three cats, a parrot, and a potbellied pig.

Author's Note

❧❧❧

THE MUSTANG is one of the most memorable symbols of the
Wild West. Even people who know very little about horses get a
thrill when they see a herd of mustangs racing free across the landscape. But these wild horses, descendants of the original mounts
that were brought over by the Spanish conquistadors, are dwindling
in numbers. All that remains of
the millions that once lived in
the western U.S. are the 50,000
wild horses and burros that
now roam in Montana, Utah,
Oregon, Nevada, California,
New Mexico, Arizona, Idaho,
Wyoming, and Colorado.
Nevada is home to more than
half of these animals.

Wild mustangs at the Born to Be Wild Mustang
Sanctuary in California.

The Bureau of Land Management is the government agency that is
responsible for the management of these wild herds. They do peri-
odic roundups of wild horses and burros to insure the health and
survival of the remaining animals on the range; they also offer some
of them for adoption. The environments where the mustangs live
are often short on forage and water. Care must be taken to make sure
that the number of horses on the range doesn't outstrip the amount
of food and water available, or starvation and death will result.

Many organizations have been formed to help protect wild mustangs and burros, and to facilitate the adoption of these animals. The following websites and phone numbers are a starting place for those who would like more information on how they can help these splendid animals.

This buckskin gelding, whose name really is Moonbeam, was rescued in Nevada by Lifesavers Wild Horse Rescue.

WEBSITES

BUREAU OF LAND MANAGEMENT
www.wildhorseandburro.blm.gov

LIFESAVERS, INC.
661-727-0049
www.wildhorserescue.org

AMERICAN MUSTANG & BURRO ASSOCIATION, INC.
530-633-9271
www.bardalisa.com

WILD HORSE SPIRIT
775-883-5488
www.wildhorsespirit.org

WILD HORSE ORGANIZED ASSISTANCE, INC. (WHOA!)
775-851-4817
www.wildhorseorganizedassistance.org